His gaze was relentless, unyielding

Trisha shivered, frightened all at once, yet at the same time very excited.

"You knew I'd come?" he demanded without preamble. "And yet you chose to wear this." His eyes savaged the nightie, and she trembled as she realized that he could see through the thin fabric to the curves of her body.

"It's midnight," she protested. "I was almost asleep."

"Eve," he said, his tone changing to a seductive taunt. "Your name should have been Eve, you play her part so well. The eternal woman, teasing, flirtatious. You have all the provocative qualities of your sex, Trisha, those that drive men to madness. Do you also have the finer qualities?"

ROSEMARY CARTER
is also the author of these

Harlequin Presents

and these

Harlequin Romances

Many of these books are available at your local bookseller.

For a free catalog listing all titles currently available,
send your name and address to:

HARLEQUIN READER SERVICE
1440 South Priest Drive, Tempe, AZ 85281
Canadian address: Stratford, Ontario N5A 6W2

ROSEMARY CARTER

daredevil

Harlequin Books

TORONTO • NEW YORK • LOS ANGELES • LONDON
AMSTERDAM • PARIS • SYDNEY • HAMBURG
STOCKHOLM • ATHENS • TOKYO • MILAN

Harlequin Presents first edition January 1983
ISBN 0-373-10560-6

Original hardcover edition published in 1982
by Mills & Boon Limited

Printed in U.S.A.

CHAPTER ONE

IT all happened so quickly. The boy riding his bicycle, whistling merrily as he careered along the road. And then the dog, darting out of the shrubbery in pursuit of a cat. Trisha Maxwell managed to jump aside just a split second before the bicycle hit the dog.

With a startled yelp it picked itself up, gave an experimental shake of legs and tail, and made off the way it had come.

The boy lay in the road. His eyes were closed, and blood was rapidly staining his clothes. With a small cry of compassion Trisha knelt down beside him.

He was breathing, she saw that at a glance, but the colour had left his face. He needed help, Trisha knew, and wished the sight of blood didn't affect her quite as much as it did.

She was wondering where to start when a car slid to a halt and a man jumped out. After bending over the boy a few moments, he said, 'He'll be all right.'

'So much blood,' Trisha said faintly.

'Have to get that stopped.' He was opening shirt buttons as he talked. In seconds he had found the wound, and was applying pressure to it. Trisha noted abstractedly that his hands were big yet gentle, the fingers long and well shaped.

'You're sure he'll be all right?' she asked after a moment.

'I think so.' The man looked up, and for the first time she saw his face. It was attractive and tanned. His eyes were blue, with laughter lines at the corners, and his hair was dark. Trisha wondered how he would look if he smiled, and felt an odd shiver quiver through her.

'You're pale too.' His voice was low and vital. 'You're not about to faint?'

'Oh no, it's just the blood. . . .'

'Worse than it looks. I'm going to ask you to press this handkerchief to the wound, while I turn his head to the side. There, that's right.' He guided her hand.

He was competent, unpanicked. He was handling the situation well, his calmness reaching to her, so that she was able to do what she had to. She should be used to the sight of blood, Trisha thought—as a child Jerry had been in one bloody scrape after another. Her brother still got into scrapes, only of a different kind. And now, as then, she had to help out.

'Do you know the child?' the man asked.

'No. I just happened to come along here when it happened. A dog ran out of the bushes. . . .'

'Have to get him to hospital.'

'His parents will be worried. . . .' Trisha began.

'Yes.' The man picked up a school-book which had fallen on to the tar. 'Identification, that's good. Timmy Broadstock. I'll get Timmy to hospital and contact his parents.'

'Is it safe to move him?'

'From the look of things I'd say yes.' Still the impression of quiet competence. 'I think Timmy's going to be all right, but he may be concussed. A doctor should have a look at him.'

'Thank God you came when you did,' Trisha said with feeling.

'You'd have managed.' He looked up at her again, and this time he was smiling, his teeth very white against the tanned face, and Trisha thought that subconsciously she had hoped his smile would be just like this. Except that it was even more attractive than she'd imagined.

'For a few moments I was afraid you might faint, but you didn't. You'd have managed just fine,' he said.

There was no reason why a smile and a few words of praise should send her heart thudding against her ribs, but they did. Trisha watched, bemused, as he stood up with the child in his arms. Till this moment she had not realised he was quite so tall. . . .

They were at the car when reality took over. 'Wait!' she called.

He turned. 'You're coming with me?'

'Oh no, I'm going to work. I just want a photo.'

Blue eyes narrowed thoughtfully. 'I don't understand.'

'Of Timmy.'

His gaze was on her face now, disturbingly intense. 'Why?'

'I'm a reporter, and. . . .'

'So you're from the press,' he interrupted her, and she saw that his smile had vanished. At the same time she noticed a relentlessness in his face which she had not caught before. The line of his jaw was strong, the planes of his cheeks chiselled. Maleness . . . from somewhere the word came into her mind.

'You want a story.'

Something in his tone brought her chin up. 'What's wrong with that?'

'I'd have liked to think you stopped to help Timmy because you were concerned.' His eyes were chips of ice.

'But I did. . . . I am. . . .' She bit her lip, confused. 'A story was the last thing on my mind when I stopped.'

'It's certainly on your mind now.'

What did he have against the press anyhow? 'We're planning a series of articles on traffic hazards. Dogs running loose are an awful hazard. That's why. . . .'

'You've made your point.' His voice was mocking as she took the little camera from her bag. 'Snap away. But only one photo, then we're off.'

Trisha angled the camera as carefully as she could, getting in as much as possible of the injured child in the man's arms. She had her story, but the photo might make more impact than words.

Throughout the man was silent. Trisha allowed herself one glance at his face, and regretted it instantly. Eyes which only minutes earlier had been lit with warmth and humour were now filled with a mockery which she did not understand.

She watched him drive away, and reproached herself for a feeling of disappointment. It did not matter that he was the most attractive man she had ever met, that she did not know his name and never would. That the few minutes of rapport had given way to disapproval. All that mattered was that Timmy Broadstock would be helped.

There was also the question of the story. Carl Samson would approve of her quick thinking even if this man had not, and she hoped he would remember her efforts when promotion was in the offing. It was important that her career get off the ground, that she get a raise. Jerry needed her help. At the thought of her brother, eyes that were as green as the sea on a spring day clouded.

The photo was clearer than she'd thought it would be, and the accompanying story was forceful. Reading it over the day after the accident, Trisha knew it was one of her best efforts. Yet a niggling dissatisfaction remained to spoil her pleasure. There was the memory of the man, of approval that had turned to bitterness at the discovery that she was from the press. Forget him, she told herself sternly, and found that was easier said than done.

'Now that's what I call a dreamboat!'

Sally, Trisha's room-mate and fellow-reporter, was staring over her shoulder at the photo. In the newspaper version only the child would be shown. But this photo was the original and in it was the man. The unsmiling look was one Trisha remembered well.

'He's divine,' Sally said.

'Is he?' Trisha spoke stiffly. 'I only noticed his arrogance.'

'Look at those gaunt cheekbones. And the eyebrows! Is he tall, Trisha? You must have noticed that.'

'He's tall.'

'What's his name?'

'I haven't the least idea.'

'Didn't you ask?'

'I suppose I should have,' Trisha said slowly. 'For the sake of the story, I mean. But he was so contemptuous. . . . Just letting me take one photo was a favour.'

'The story nothing!' Sally was laughing incredulously. 'Though that would have been a good enough excuse. Trisha Maxwell, this macho type must be the best-looking man you've come across in all your twenty-three years, and you let him get away without even asking his name!'

'He was so damn supercilious I was glad to see the back of him,' Trisha insisted, and remembered that until the moment she'd said she was a reporter he had not been arrogant and supercilious at all.

'Burt Lancaster and Robert Redford in one,' Sally went on as if she had not registered the protest. 'Oh well, Trisha dear, when you've settled with some nice meek man—George perhaps?—and begun to raise a brood of kids, I just hope you won't regret what you let slip away.'

'George *is* nice. And not in the downgraded way you keep painting him.' With unnecessary force Trisha pulled a fresh sheet of paper through her typewriter. 'What's more, I have no intention of getting married right now. To anybody.' She looked up and saw the gleam of laughter in her friend's eyes. 'What I do have slipping away is a deadline. Move it, Sally!'

'Trisha?' The voice on the phone sounded anxious.

'Jerry? Jerry, I told you not to phone me at work.'

'Trish, it's important. I have to talk to you.'

Her eyes on the typed page in front of her, Trisha struck a pen through a sentence that seemed out of place. With her mind only half on her brother, she said into the phone, 'Jerry, I have a deadline.'

'Trisha, I need more money. Saunders has given me an ultimatum.'

The despair in her brother's voice got through to her. Switching off her typewriter, Trisha asked, 'How much more?'

'Five hundred.'

'Five hundred? Jerry, you promised!'

'I know. Trish, I'm sorry, and it won't happen again. I promise.'

'You say that every time. . . .'

'I mean it—honest! Trish, I have to have that money.'

He did need it, Trisha knew. The fact that Jerry had let himself be drawn into another harebrained scheme was quite apart from the fact that unless he could bail himself out of it he would be in serious trouble. Pushing a distraught hand through hair that was the colour of molten copper, she said, 'That's a lot of money. Jerry, that's really a lot of money.'

'I know. And I feel bad about it. But you will manage, won't you, Trish? You always do.'

She always did, Trisha acknowledged to herself, registering the boyish coaxing in her brother's tone. Somehow she always did.

'Would you be so irresponsible if you didn't keep banking on me to come through?' she asked, voicing the question that had been in her mind for some time.

'You don't think I got into this mess purposely?' He was reproachful. 'And I have said it won't happen again.'

'Forget it,' she said wearily. Jerry did not get into trouble on purpose, at least not consciously. And it *would* happen again, it would go on happening, for that was his nature. Just as she would go on helping him, for nurturing Jerry had become a habit ever since their parents had been killed in a motor accident seven years ago, leaving sixteen-year-old Trisha and Jerry, three years younger, to fend for themselves.

'I'll do my best,' she said, 'but it won't be easy. I don't happen to have five hundred lying around.'

She was frowning unhappily as she put down the phone and attacked the typewriter with renewed vigour. If only she could wangle a raise, but for the moment any increase in her salary seemed remote.

Just half an hour later came the summons to see Carl Samson, editor-in-chief of the paper. It seemed almost telepathic.

'Have a seat, Miss Maxwell.' Mr Samson, middle-aged and ruddy-faced, had a gruff voice and manner that daunted many a cub reporter. At the moment he was smiling. Trisha, who had tensed at his call, relaxed.

'Good article you did yesterday. Good picture.'

'I just happened to be on the scene,' Trisha said breathlessly.

'Quick thinking nevertheless. Like that in a new kid. You have the makings of a fine reporter.'

Trisha glowed at his words. 'I'm glad you called me in to tell me.'

'Didn't call you in just for that.' Carl Samson sat forward, elbows on the desk, one hand playing with a pencil. 'How would you like a special assignment, Miss Maxwell?'

'I'd like that!'

'Hm.' A searching gaze took in green eyes that were wide and excited in an oval face framed by copper curls. Possessed of a body that was as lovely as her face, Trisha was accustomed to having men look at her. But Carl Samson's scrutiny, male though it was, was also shrewd and assessing.

'Very suitable,' he murmured, as if to himself. And then, before Trisha had time to wonder what he meant, he asked, 'What do you know of the Vareen case?'

'The kidnapping?'

'The same.'

'What everyone knows. Paulie Vareen was kidnapped. She was hidden for two weeks. Her return. . . .' Trisha's words died away, as she looked curiously at her superior. 'That's all been covered.'

'The facts, yes. Nobody has spoken to Paulie Vareen.'

His tone was gruff, dry, nothing in it to make Trisha excited. Yet the eyes that stared into his were shining. 'You want. . . . You don't mean you want me to interview Paulie Vareen?'

'Exactly what I do want.'

'That's incredible!' Trisha breathed. 'You're sending me. . . . above Sally and Barb . . . they're much more experienced.'

'I know that.' Drily.

Don't blink your eyes at a miracle. From somewhere the words of the Irish grandmother who had long departed this world came to her mind. Don't ask too many questions. Snatch the opportunity and ponder the wherefores later.

And yet the question emerged nevertheless, 'Because of the way I handled the story of the accident?'

'Partly.' Flint-grey eyes were even shrewder than before. 'It did prove your competence. More especially that you can make the most of a situation.'

Trisha did not know that she was sitting on the edge of her chair. 'You said partly. . . .'

'Right. Before I go into the particular qualities that make you suitable for this assignment, suppose I tell you more about it. Miss Maxwell, the reason that Paulie Vareen has not been interviewed is that no reporter can get within a mile of her. Raoul Vareen, her guardian—her brother too, as it happens—has the gates of Vareen House barred to the press.'

'Why?'

'He has a long-standing feud with the media.'

Momentarily an image swam into Trisha's mind—a lean face, rugged and devastatingly handsome. Quickly she pushed it from her; this was not the moment to dwell on a man she would never see again. She needed all her concentration to digest what Carl Samson was saying.

A little uncertainly, she said, 'You did say you want me to interview Paulie Vareen.'

'It will be a scoop for *Contemporary*. For you as well.'

A once-in-a-lifetime scoop for a junior reporter. Adrenalin pumped through her veins as she realised what the opportunity could mean for her.

'How will I get past the gates of Vareen House?' She smiled suddenly, her face crinkling in a way which many men, George Tomlinson among them, found irresistible. 'Break my way in with a blunderbuss?'

'With your looks.'

'I beg your pardon!' She had been joking. It startled her to see that Carl was serious.

'There's a younger brother, Gary Vareen— mid-twenties, falls in love at the sight of a pretty face.'

'Mr Samson. . . .' she began.

'You're a very beautiful young woman, Miss Maxwell. I believe you'd be just his type.'

As simple as that. The particular qualities that made her suitable for a reporting assignment. If Trisha had not been so amazed she would have been outraged.

It took her a few seconds to catch her breath. Then she said, 'I'm not about to marry a stranger. Not even for a scoop.'

'Who said anything about marriage? Gary Vareen falls out of love as quickly as he plunges into it.'

'An affair, then. A liaison.' Trisha wished she could stop herself blushing, but she could not. 'I . . . I'm seeing somebody. And anyway, I . . . I'm not the kind of person who. . . .' She stopped. In her own ears she sounded silly.

'. . . . hops into bed at the first date,' Mr Samson finished the sentence for her. 'You're the kind who needs everything tied up and legal.' He shrugged. 'That's your business. There's to be a party next week—Madame Lovanne. . . . Gary Vareen will be there. You'll be there too. You'll make it your business to meet him. You'll flatter him, he likes that. Chances are good that he'll ask you to spend a weekend at Vareen House.'

He had it all so pat. 'And once there I'll interview Paulie,' Trisha said, amazed at Carl's cool calculation.

'Right.' Calm, assured, as if everything was settled.

Trisha raised questioning eyes. 'Even supposing I could pull it off, from what you say of Raoul Vareen, I can't imagine he would let a reporter into the house.'

'Chances are he won't be there. Raoul Vareen's business affairs keep him pretty much on the go. But you wouldn't be coming in as a reporter. You'd let it be known you're a model.' And as Trisha stared, 'With your looks you'd be believed.'

Uncomfortably, she shifted in her chair. 'I can't do it,' she said at last.

Across the desk from her one eyebrow lifted in a face that was craggy and hard-bitten.

'It's . . . well, it's not honest.' Again the image of the man who'd helped Timmy Broadstock came into her mind. 'It . . . it doesn't seem right.'

Carl's pencil tapped on the smooth walnut surface of the desk. After a moment he said, 'It's not all that bad. And financially you'd do very well out of it.' After Trisha had let out an involuntary gasp at the figure he named, he went on, 'I've heard—via the grapevine—that you could do with the extra money.'

Was there anything that escaped the man's notice?

'I couldn't write anything confidential,' Trisha said low-toned.

'All I want are the facts. Some personal recollections, a few photos. . . .' Another shrewd glance. 'Along with providing us with a scoop you'd be advancing your career with a speed you could never manage otherwise.' If you don't do it'—he spread his hands—'it's not always easy to leave the bottom rung. But I suppose you know that, my dear.'

'I . . . I don't look like a model. . . .' Trisha

protested, hating him, yet thinking of Jerry at the same time.

'With the right clothes you will. You have the face and the figure, the bearing. . . . Say the word, and you'll go shopping tomorrow.' He stood up, and Trisha understood that the interview was over. 'Let me know what you decide,' said Carl as she made for the door.

'Will you come? Please?'

It was impossible not to like the young man with the laughing eyes and the appealing manner.

'I'll have to think about it.' She smiled at him. 'Who else will be there?'

'If you're thinking of a chaperone—are you?— my sister will be there. Paulie's been through a lot.' Momentarily blue eyes clouded. 'A little friendly female company is just what she needs.'

Damn you, Carl Samson. If I'd met this nice Gary Vareen without any contrivance I might be tempted to accept the invitation despite George's probable objections.

'Please,' he said again, into the silence. 'That glass of champagne spilling on my suit couldn't have been just an accident.'

I've seen others flirting, Trisha thought as she threw him a glance from beneath lashes that would have been the envy of many a genuine model. I never thought it was in my nature to do it myself.

'What was it, then?' she asked on a bubble of laughter.

'Fate,' Gary said solemnly, though his eyes

were still smiling. 'A trick of fate if ever I saw it.'

A trick inspired by Carl Samson. Feeling thoroughly disgusted, she opened her mouth to refuse Gary Vareen's invitation. And then Jerry came to mind. His call last night, the note of despair in his tone as he'd said, 'I *must* have that money, Trish. I could be in awful trouble if I don't. . . .' A plea that was wilder than any that had preceded it.

'*Will* you come for the weekend?' asked the man at her side.

It was not easy to maintain the flirtatious smile as she looked up at him. 'That sounds lovely,' she said.

Carl was delighted with the news of her achievement. So much so that he was prepared to give her an advance on her month's salary, enough money to placate Jerry's creditors for a short while.

'I knew you could do it,' he beamed. 'Getting an entrée into Vareen House was the biggest difficulty. The actual story will be a piece of cake compared to that. Go to it, girl!'

Which, quite literally, was what she was doing, Trisha thought three days later, as Gary's red sports car sped up the long driveway of the Vareen estates.

She was very quiet as the car took the bends of the drive with a young man's love of speed. The estate was bigger than anything she had imagined. The drive was lined with oaks, as the outer wall had been. On each side were orchards, the trees heavy with peaches and apricots and mangoes, the

tropical fruits of Natal. And then the orchards
gave way to velvet-smooth lawns and flowerbeds
rioting with colour, and at the end of the drive
stood Vareen House itself. It was the loveliest
house Trisha had ever seen, also, surely, one of
the biggest.

She cast a quick look at Gary, and felt fear flut-
ter inside her. Who are you, Gary Vareen? You
look so young and eager and filled with life and
fun. Are you also conscious of your status? Or has
living amidst such magnificence made no impression on you? Above all, will I cope?

'Don't let the place awe you,' Gary said cheer-
fully, as if he guessed at the thoughts passing
through her head and wanted to dispel them.

'It is rather awesome,' she said slowly.

'As long as you don't think it awful,' he
quipped. The car slowed as a hand reached out
and covered one of hers. 'I just want you to enjoy
yourself.'

'I'm sure I will.' It was hard to smile through
the inevitable stab of guilt.

They walked through an entrance hall with a
high vaulted ceiling and a marble floor, and Gary
stopped at the bottom of a lovely winding staircase
and called, 'Paulie! I'm back.'

Moments later a girl was running down the
stairs. She was wearing jeans and her long fair
hair was brushed back in a ponytail. She smiled
shyly as Gary made the introductions, but Trisha
saw that her face was pale, and when the smile
vanished there was a haunted look in the blue
eyes.

'Hello, Trisha,' said the girl whom every reporter in Natal wanted to photograph. 'I'm so glad you decided to come.'

'Been lonely, little sister?' This from Gary, and Trisha saw the look of affection that passed between them.

'Yes. I've been looking forward to the weekend.' And then, with another wan look at Trisha, 'I've been dying for some company.'

'Let's have tea at the pool,' Gary suggested.

'When I've shown Trisha her room. It's next to mine.' She was turning away when she said, 'Oh, by the way, Raoul just phoned. He's coming down too.'

The strict older brother. Trisha tensed; she'd been counting on his absence. Casting a quick glance at Gary, she saw that his expression was set.

'Oh, really?' he said, and the alert ear of the reporter registered the strain in his casualness.

'He knows about Trisha. Relax, Gary, I'm sure he won't mind. It's just the press he objects to.'

'Yes, well. . . .' Gary paused uncertainly a moment before saying, 'Meet you at the pool in ten minutes.'

Questions tumbled on Trisha's lips as she accompanied Paulie down a long passageway with carpeting as soft as feathers underfoot. Her curiosity was not just that of a reporter with a job to do, but the natural interest of one who found herself in an unusual setting. Somehow she managed to stifle the questions. It was still too soon. . . .

She followed Paulie through a doorway and

stood quite still as impressions of the room swept over her. Lovely rosewood furniture, the lines sleek and modern, the wood vividly glowing. Curtains and bedspread in a woven fabric, cool blues and greens blending in perfect harmony.

Trisha had a brief vision of the tiny apartment near the Durban sea-front which she shared with Sally. Turning back to Paulie, she breathed, 'This is beautiful. You have such a lovely home.'

'. . . . Yes,' Paulie said wanly. 'Thank you.'

You poor girl! None of this means very much to you. Or at least not at the moment. Perhaps you'd even prefer my tiny apartment and the freedom that goes with it.

'Gary said something about the pool. . . .'

'Yes. Do you have a bikini?' And as Trisha nodded, 'Oh good. The pool's on the west lawn. You can't miss it.'

Gary and Paulie were at the pool when she got there. Gary was swimming. Paulie, also wearing a bikini, was oiling her shoulders. She looked very thin—too thin. Had she lost much weight during her ordeal? Trisha wondered.

Trisha took off her rose-coloured towelling wrap to reveal the matching bikini underneath. Her mirror image had told her that the garment flattered her slim tanned figure. As it should have. She had never spent so much money on clothes in her life. And yet, while the sight of herself looking her best was satisfying, her greater emotion had been one of resentment.

'Look at what you're getting out of this deal,' Sally had said just a day earlier, looking at the clothes laid out on Trisha's bed.

'Lovely clothes—I know. And I'd be ecstatic if I'd bought them with money I'd earned myself. But this was a blank cheque Carl handed me. . . .'

'I know what you're trying to say. But what's the difference? You've been given a once-in-a-lifetime opportunity . . . Vareen House, my golly! Enjoy it.'

'I'm not getting through to you, Sally. I can only tell you I'll be glad to get back into my own clothes.'

Watching Gary turn an under-water somersault at the far end of the pool, Trisha tried to put the conversation out of her mind. Perhaps she was being unduly sensitive, as Sally and Carl had suggested. In any event, for better or worse she was at Vareen House now; she might as well make the best of it.

The sun was in her eyes, and she turned slightly, the movement revealing Paulie from a new angle. Trisha stifled a gasp as she saw the ugly sore on the girl's left foot.

'What happened?' Her voice was warm with concern.

A hand moved to cover the spot as if Paulie's instinctive reaction was one of shame. After a moment she dropped the shielding hand. The eyes that lifted to Trisha's were clouded.

'They burnt me.'

'No!' The exclamation of distress was genuine.

'The men. . . . You . . . you know about them, don't you?'

'The kidnappers,' Trisha said softly.

'The kidnappers,' Paulie agreed painfully.
'They . . . burnt me, with a cigarette. . . .'

It was known that Paulie Vareen had been badly
treated, but the details had never been disclosed.
And now Paulie seemed about to talk of them
voluntarily. Not an hour at Vareen House, and
already some of the facts Carl wanted so badly
were within Trisha's grasp.

She touched her towelling bag. Inside it was a
camera in the shape of a cigarette lighter. A photo
of the injured foot would be the simplest task
Trisha had ever accomplished.

She did not know what made her say, 'You
don't have to talk about it.'

'I think I want to talk,' Paulie said slowly. 'I
brood about it all day. And at night. . . .' She
paused, blue eyes shimmering with tears.
'Sometimes I think I'll never forget what
happened.'

'It was so bad, then?'

'It was awful. They all want to know about it.
Reporters. . . .'

'I'd heard you don't give interviews.'

'I don't. Raoul says. . . . Raoul won't allow a
reporter into the grounds.'

Warmth flooded Trisha's cheeks. She could feel
it creeping along her neck. Straight reporting was
one thing, but this was quite another. She looked
at the small gentle girl at her side and wished she
was anywhere but at Vareen House.

'Your brother feels the press shouldn't cover
the story?' she asked in a low tone.

'Raoul hates the press. Sometimes I think. . . .'

She stopped, and Trisha saw that she was eyeing the sore once more. 'They burnt me deliberately,' she went on unsteadily.

Don't say any more! I don't want to hear it. Not like this, in this underhand manner. I am going back to Carl and I am going to tell him that I won't undertake this assignment. And to heck with the consequences!

'Paulie. . . .' she began.

'They wanted details of Raoul's business affairs,' Paulie went on, as if she had not heard the interruption. 'I said I didn't know them. . . .'

Trisha swallowed. 'Why are you telling me all this?'

'I like you. Gary's had so many girl-friends—but you're different, somehow.'

'You don't know me,' protested Trisha. 'We've just met.'

'All the same, I can tell. Something about your eyes. . . . You *are* different.'

If you only knew quite how different! Now was the time to leave, before this very trusting young girl began to confide a story, the telling of which she would later regret. Gary was making his way to the edge of the pool, waving his arm in an exuberant gesture as he reached the side.

'Coming in, girls?' His voice was friendly, eager.

'Not right now.' Paulie laughed at him, and Trisha saw again that there was ease and affection between brother and sister. 'We're talking.'

'Girl talk?' Gary had clambered out of the pool, and stood beside them, droplets of water falling from his body on to the hot stone.

'I was just starting to tell Trisha about my foot
... what happened. . . .'

The smile left Gary's face. 'Paulie. . . .'

'It's what I want,' his sister said quickly. 'I feel
I can talk to Trisha. She's nice.'

'She *is* nice,' Gary agreed, squatting down and
putting an arm around Trisha's shoulders. 'I'm
rather partial to Trisha myself.'

'So I see,' a low voice drawled from behind
them.

'Raoul!'

As Paulie's exclamation burst out, Trisha sat
very still. The muscles had bunched in her stomach, and her neck had gone rigid. She had heard
that voice before. A deep voice, vibrant and sexy.
There could not be another one quite like it. Oh
no, she thought, it can't be! I'm imagining things.

CHAPTER TWO

'HI, Raoul,' said Gary. 'You're back early.'

'And you could have done with staying at the office a little later. Aren't you going to introduce me to your friend?'

The few moments had given Trisha a small measure of control. She took a breath and looked up into the face of the man who towered above them all.

It *was* him. Foolish that she had let herself think even for a moment that she might have made a mistake about his voice. The eyes of the man who had helped the injured Timmy Broadstock were on her face, blue, a steel-like blue, probing her face with an intensity that made her think that he could see through to the inner core of her being. Which was clearly absurd.

'Trisha, my brother Raoul. Raoul, my friend Trisha Maxwell.'

Would he refer to their previous meeting? Did he in fact remember her? Trisha's mouth had gone so dry that she could not speak. Wordlessly she stared up into a face that was hard and gauntly male.

'How do you do, Miss Maxwell?' His voice was as low and as lazy as before. He had forgotten!

Forcing a smile, she said, 'Hello, Mr Vareen.'

'Raoul—Trisha.' Gary sounded suddenly very

young. 'No formalities, please!'

'Suits me. Paulie said you were bringing a friend. Have you known each other long?'

'Just four days. We met at Madame Lovanne's party—a matter of champagne spilling over my suit. Poor girl, she was so upset. Didn't realise that the accident was fortuitous, without it we'd never have met.'

'How accidents have a way of bringing people together,' a dry voice murmured.

Gary did not appear to register the flush that suffused Trisha's cheeks. 'It really was the most marvellous luck,' he rushed on. 'Trisha's a model, Raoul.'

Sensuous lips slanted in a mocking grin. 'Now why didn't I guess?'

'I'm surprised you didn't.' The mockery was lost on Gary too. 'Just look at her face . . . her figure . . . Isn't she gorgeous?'

Trisha forced herself to be very still as she was subjected to a scrutiny that was particularly and very blatantly male. The bikini was as brief as it had been expensive. The eyes that raked her body, lingering outrageously on the high swell of her breasts, on the smallness of her waist, on thighs that were long and smooth, told her that she might as well be wearing nothing at all.

'Gorgeous,' Raoul agreed blandly. And then, addressing himself to Trisha in a voice that was the utmost in politeness, 'Have you been modelling long?'

She forced herself to meet his gaze. 'A while.'

'I believe you're being modest.' His eyes

gleamed. 'Only those at the top of their particular poles are invited to parties at Madame Lovanne.' He paused, a very brief pause. 'And those who have influence of some sort.'

'Raoul!' Paulie protested before Trisha could speak. 'You're not being very friendly to our guest.'

'I do apologise. I hope you'll enjoy your time here, Trisha. A top-flight model keeps such long hours, you must be exhausted.'

'Raoul?' Gary was frowning, his friendly young countenance uneasy in the face of a baiting which he sensed but did not understand. 'Raoul, Paulie's right—you are being rude.'

'I'm never rude to welcome guests.' Trisha wondered if only she heard the emphasis on the word 'welcome'. 'All I'm trying to say is, and I'm sure Trisha understands'—white teeth showed against the tan in a dangerous smile—'that I hope she will relax. That any thought of—work— should be the last thing on her mind.'

Trisha's heart was beating uncomfortably fast against her ribs. Just minutes ago she had been thinking of a way to leave Vareen House with the least fuss possible, but Raoul Vareen's appearance had made that impossible. He was playing with her, taunting her. Without hurting Gary and Paulie, a thing she could not bring herself to do, her defences were limited. Still, she would show him that she would not allow herself to be intimidated.

She lifted her chin in a manner that would indicate battle to those who knew her well. 'Don't

worry about me, Raoul. I intend to make the most
of my stay.'

There was a look from eyes that were too perceptive, an unnerving look that caused Trisha to
curl her fingers into her palms to stop her hands
from trembling. But there was no answer. None
was necessary. She and Raoul understood each
other, and the situation, perfectly.

He was going to change, Raoul announced, then
he'd be back for a swim. Trisha sat rigid, refusing
to watch the tall lithe figure go towards the house.
She was not aware that her tension showed till
she heard Gary say, 'Don't let my brother get to
you.'

She composed her face before turning to him.
'He didn't get to me.'

'He will. He's a devil with women.' Gary looked
unhappy, and Trisha sensed that he would have
given much to keep his brother away from Vareen
House this weekend. Not as much as she herself
would have given, she thought.

'I can stand my own with Raoul,' she said
lightly. 'I think I'll swim.'

Gary and Paulie joined her in the pool. Amidst
much lighthearted clowning and splashing they
appeared to have forgotten Raoul. But she would
not forget him, Trisha knew as she joined in the
water-play. She would be aware of him every
minute of her stay at Vareen House. And even
afterwards came the appalling whisper in the farthest reaches of her mind.

They were sunbathing again when Raoul re-
appeared in dark blue swimming-trunks. Trisha

was unable to stop her eyes from going to him, and at the same moment her heart gave an odd jerk.

He was all male, utterly and compellingly male. The clean chiselled lines of his face were repeated in his body. His shoulders were broad, his chest strong, his hips narrow. His legs were very long, the thighs powerful, the calves muscled in the manner of one who spent much of his time out of doors, an impression that was reinforced by his smooth bronze tan.

Involuntarily, against her will almost, she looked up at his face. She felt as if a force she was powerless to resist had drawn her gaze to his. He was watching her, his eyes narrowed. Swept with an odd primeval longing, Trisha shuddered, and saw the blue eyes light with satisfaction. A devil with women, Gary had said, and in no way unaware of his appeal. Damn the man! Damn Raoul Vareen for making her feel more vulnerable than she had ever felt in her life.

He seemed to tower above her, standing so close to her that she felt giddy all at once. With an effort she pulled her eyes from his face and dropped them beneath her lashes. For a moment she felt better, and then she was feeling giddy once more, for now her gaze was focused on his legs, and as if mesmerised she stared at the dark hairs curling on the strong calves and thighs.

He laughed, the sound low and amused. Darting a quick glance at Gary and Paulie, Trisha realised that the sound had been so soft that they had not heard it. She felt her cheeks grow warm once more.

It was with relief that she saw Raoul move to the pool. He took the water in a clean swift dive, then, surfacing, he began to swim, his arms moving in strokes that looked effortlessly powerful.

A little wildly Trisha glanced about her. More than ever she wished she could leave Vareen House. The reluctance she had felt all along in regard with the assignment had become even stronger. Surely Paulie had the right to privacy. The girl was shy and reserved. Galling as it was to admit that Raoul could be right about anything, she knew that he was right to keep the media away from his sister. Paulie might find interviews and the resulting articles an ordeal. Looking at the haunted blue eyes, at the festering mark on the thin foot, she knew that the girl had suffered enough.

Getting away from Vareen House would also mean getting away from Raoul, and Trisha wanted just that. The fact that her job might be in jeopardy, that Jerry would not get the money he needed, seemed secondary to the alarming impact Raoul Vareen made on her peace of mind.

'Gary, we have to talk,' she began jerkily.

'Why, sure, Trisha. What is it?'

'It's about. . . .' She stopped as a maid arrived at the pool, and said to Gary, 'Phone-call from Miss Yvonne.'

As Gary rose reluctantly to his feet and made for the house, Trisha wondered if the call had come at the right moment. Her words had been impulsive. She had begun to talk without knowing quite what she would say, and how it should be said. Without knowing if either Gary or Paulie would find it in their hearts to forgive her. Knowing that she cared how they felt even after so short an acquaintance.

She glanced at the pool where a bronzed figure was carving the water. At least there was no need to wonder about the matter of Raoul's forgiveness; it would not be forthcoming. But that did not matter, she told herself fiercely. She wanted nothing, expected nothing, from Raoul Vareen.

'What are the colours for summer?' Paulie asked.

'Colours?' Turning her head, Trisha looked at the girl through a blur. 'Oh, fashion colours. . . .' She had done a write-up of a minor fashion show just a few weeks ago. 'Pastels are strong,' she said. 'Pinks, lilac, primrose.' And then, managing a smile as she focused on Paulie's face, 'I would think lilac would be just lovely with your complexion.'

With Gary in the house and Raoul in the water the two girls were able to talk uninterruptedly. Girl-talk, as Gary had laughingly called it. Paulie was interested in fashion and movies and pop music. She had been through an ordeal that would have drained many a stronger person, and she was now back in a home the splendour of which the press would make much of—if allowed—nevertheless she was absorbed in the same interests as her contemporaries.

Once Trisha let her eyes go to the water. Raoul

had reached the far side of the pool and had let his feet touch ground. For a moment their glances locked. His lips curved in the mocking smile which Trisha was getting to know so well.

It seemed that having started to talk, Paulie was enjoying herself so much that she did not want to stop. Eyes that were haunted in repose were now bright with enthusiasm. Cheeks were flushed with a colour not put there by the short time in the sun. It came to Trisha that Paulie, for all the riches and luxuries with which she was surrounded, was a very lonely person. A little despairingly she wondered what effect her confession would have. Would it send Paulie scurrying back into the unhappy shell she had so obviously created for herself?

Gary returned, and Paulie asked, 'What did Yvonne want?'

'She thought we could get together.' He sat down close beside Trisha. 'I told her some other time.'

'She won't have liked that.'

'She didn't.' Was there a note of truculence in Gary's tone as he put his hand on Trisha's knee? 'Trisha, there was something you wanted to talk about. . . .'

'Nothing important.' She said it lightly, and wondered if the hand on her knee was part of Carl's plan. It made her feel uncomfortable, and she was not sure why.

'But you said. . . .

'Not right now, Gary.'

The phone call had given her time to think.

Her intention to leave Vareen House without any attempt to ask Paulie for details of the kidnapping had not changed. She would go just as soon as she possibly could. But she could not blurt out the truth as she had so nearly done. Paulie would be shattered, and Gary, as appealing a young man as she had met in a long while, would be very hurt. She owed it to them both to make her departure gentle.

'The modelling world must be fascinating,' Raoul said at dinner.

Trisha shot him a provocative glance. 'Oh, it is.'

'You really must tell us more about it.'

'Plenty of time to do that,' she said smilingly, refusing to rise to his bait. 'I'd hate to be a bore.'

'You could never be that!' Gary exclaimed. 'Don't you think Trisha's the most fascinating girl you've met in a long time, Raoul?'

'Certainly the most intriguing,' came the soft reply. The words were directed at Gary, but the raising of an eyebrow was solely for Trisha; she knew that she alone had seen it.

'This is going to be the best weekend we've had in so long,' Paulie put in happily. 'Raoul and Gary, both of you here—and Trisha. I can't remember when I've felt so good.'

'I'm glad, Paulie.'

The last statement came from Raoul, the words spoken in a soft tone. The double-entendre of the past few minutes had left Trisha with an unsteady pulse-beat. She had resolved not to look at Raoul if she could help it, for each time he was waiting for her, and as their eyes met she was conscious of shock waves shooting through her system. Now, however, the softness of his tone pulled her gaze back to him.

He was smiling at his sister, and the mockery that seemed reserved only for Trisha was missing. The smile that curved his lips extended to his eyes, warming them, bringing back a memory of how he had looked that first time, at the accident, in those minutes before he had discovered that Trisha was a reporter.

He's human, Trisha thought. He's arrogant and far too sure of himself, but he's human. He will always show kindness to those he loves—Paulie, the sister who has suffered so much, Gary, the brother who looks up to him while knowing that he can never emulate him. His wife, when he marries. . . . She found she had to push the last thought from her.

Right now Raoul's concern was obviously for Paulie. He was no fool. He knew Trisha's purpose in coming to Vareen House in the guise of a model, and she was as sure as she could be that he would not let her get away with it. But the fact that he had thus far said nothing to reveal the truth indicated that he would handle the matter in his own way, sparing both Paulie and Gary as much distress as he could. His sister was re-cuperating from an ordeal. He did not want her to suffer the disillusionment of discovering that someone she had taken to was a fraud.

He was talking to Paulie still, and it was safe to

observe him. He was all long rangy male, Trisha thought. A white polo-necked sweater clung to his body, revealing the muscled breadth of his shoulders and enhancing his tan. Navy slacks, well cut and tight, looked superb on the long legs. His hair was dark and glossy, his eyes a deep midnight blue in the artificial light of the room. His lips curved at the corners, deepening the laughter lines etched around his mouth. Trisha stared at the lips as if mesmerised, unable to stop herself wondering how it would feel to be kissed by him, and thinking at the same time that he had the dangerous look of a jungle animal.

He turned his head quite suddenly, catching her off her guard. A gleam came into the eyes that held hers, defying them to shift away. He knows what I was thinking, Trisha thought wildly. It's absurd that he could know, but he does!

Controlling a shudder, she directed her attention to her plate. It seemed the safest place for her to look. She let the conversation at the table wash over her, managing somehow to produce the correct answers when called on to do so. She heard Paulie talk, Gary laugh. They were like figures in a movie, acting out their parts, yet somehow insubstantial. Her awareness was focused on Raoul, and there was nothing insubstantial about him at all.

'Potatoes,' Paulie said once, and there was a shudder in her voice. 'I wonder if I'll ever be able to look at a boiled potato without thinking of the kidnapping.'

'Sure you will,' Gary said soothingly.

'But meal after meal. . . . Did I tell you. . . .'

'You did, dear.' Raoul cut in quietly. 'By the way, did you get to watch the programme on ceramics last night?'

'Yes,' Paulie said eagerly, 'I did.'

'Was it any good?'

'Very. I picked up some new ideas on dyes. . . .'

Trisha did not listen as the younger girl chattered about a hobby which was evidently very close to her heart. Her mind was on Raoul, on the effortless way in which he had managed to stop his sister from launching into the very topic which would be of interest to the reporter who had inveigled her way into Vareen House. So easily had he manipulated the conversation that neither Gary nor Paulie seemed aware of what he had done. A little wryly Trisha wondered how Raoul intended to manipulate the situation for the remainder of the weekend. Futile speculation, for tomorrow, after making a suitable excuse that would satisfy both Gary and Paulie, she would be gone from here. Raoul of course would see through the excuse, but overriding his contempt would be his relief at seeing the last of her.

She was relieved when the evening ended at last. 'What about a walk before turning in?' Gary suggested.

'I'd really like to go to bed.'

He looked disappointed. 'I've hardly had a minute alone with you all day.'

Trisha glanced at Raoul. He was sitting back in a velvet-upholstered armchair, one leg leaning nonchalantly over the other, the long rangy figure in a pose of utter relaxation. And it *was* a pose, Trisha knew. His expression was as relaxed as his body, but the eyes that held hers were anything but relaxed. They were narrowed and alert.

You don't want me to go with Gary, Trisha thought, looking into the face of the man who disturbed her more than she cared to admit. You think it's enough that your expression should tell me so. That I should be intimidated by your wishes.

Rebellion surged within her. I will not let your arrogant manner frighten me, Raoul Vareen. I do what *I* want. And if I wanted to walk with Gary I'd do just that.

But she did not want to walk in the scented moonlight with nice Gary Vareen. It came to her that she wanted to walk with Raoul. She stared at him, her breathing slightly shallow now, and saw a sudden gleam light the dark eyes. He knows, came the appalling thought. Just as he knew that I wondered about his kisses. Dear God, the man is like some magician of old. He can see right through me.

'Trisha?' said Gary, pleadingly.

'Not tonight.' She was *not* intimidated by Raoul, she told herself again. But the moment of reckoning was yet to come. No way she could avoid it. And the sooner it was faced, the sooner she could leave this place.

'It's been a lovely evening,' she said, smiling at the younger man. 'A lovely day altogether. Thank you, Gary. But I really think I should go to my room now.'

She was not surprised when she heard the soft knock at the door. She had made no move to get undressed and go to bed. Instead she had been sitting at the open window, staring out over a garden silvered by moonlight, waiting for him.

She would keep the meeting short, she decided. What needed saying could be said in a few minutes. Above all, she would not let herself be affected by him. It was this last which would be the most difficult, she knew almost immediately, as he stepped into the room and closed the door very quietly behind him.

In the dim light of the bedside lamp his impact was more devastating than ever. Everything about him seemed enhanced and exaggerated. He looked taller, more powerful, infinitely more dangerous than he had done in the very ordinary setting of a family dinner. The aura he gave off was purely sexual, Trisha thought wildly, noting the superb body clothed in figure-moulding clothes. There was something devilish in the sardonic set of sensuous lips, in the high gaunt cheekbones, and the mobility of winging brows. Devilish and at the same time dynamically attractive. Involuntarily she took a step towards him, drawn by an appeal that was greater than anything she had ever imagined.

His lips curved, and in the soft light she saw his eyes glitter, and with the sight sanity returned.

Just in time. Drawing herself up to her full height—how little five feet and six inches appeared in the shade of six feet two—she stepped back, tilted her chin, and said, 'You want to talk, I suppose.'

'What did you think I wanted?' he asked, very politely.

Damn him, he knew how she felt. He'd known all evening.

'A rhetorical question,' she replied with all the dignity at her command. 'Okay, let's have it—the condemnation, the command to get going.'

'Sounds like a one-sided conversation.' He seemed amused.

'I'm not in the mood for your sarcasm. Just say what you have to.'

'I hardly think you're in a position to give orders.' The amusement vanished, to be replaced by mockery. 'All right then, let's skip the preamble. We both know why you're here.'

'You . . . you're very angry, aren't you?' She did not know what made her say it, why his anger mattered quite as much as it did.

'Angry?' He shrugged. 'Disgusted would be a better word.'

You shouldn't have asked me to do this, Carl. You knew I didn't want to.

'I know you've no time for the press,' she said slowly.

'Two bad experiences in the past were enough to put me off.' His voice was icy. 'I don't surprise easily, Trisha Maxwell, but I confess even I didn't expect you'd stoop quite so low.'

Through dry lips Trisha said, 'I didn't want to do it.'

'Come on,' he drawled.

'Really.'

'I suppose,' he said contemptuously, his eyes never leaving her face, 'that the whole thing is just one colossal coincidence. You have a dual career—high-class fashion model Mondays, Wednesdays and Fridays, high-minded reporter the rest of the week.'

'You don't need to be so sarcastic,' she whispered painfully.

'I also suppose,' he went on, as smoothly as if he had not registered her distress, 'that you just happened to be at the same party as Gary, and that you just happened to spill champagne on his suit.'

'What do you want me to say?' she asked in a low voice, hating him.

'There isn't much *to* say.' The contempt had left him, and now his tone was without expression. 'Is there?'

He took a step towards her. Trisha took a hasty step back and found a dresser blocking her escape. The room seemed almost at once claustrophobic.

'Did you really think you could get away with it?'

'I. . . .' Her mouth was so dry that it was difficult to speak. Go, she pleaded silently. Don't you feel the vibrations in this room? There's anger here, but there's something sexual too, and it's making me feel so confused.

'Well?' he demanded harshly.

'I thought. . . .' A small pink tongue went out

to moisten her lips. 'That is. . . . I could have got away with it.'

A new expression came into his face, a look of sudden understanding. 'You didn't expect me to be here.'

'No. Carl Samson, my editor, said you'd be away. Besides, I didn't know. . . .' She stopped.

The look of understanding deepened. 'You didn't know who I was. We never did get to find out each other's names. I'd forgotten that.'

'We would have. But you were angry. You'd discovered I was a reporter.'

'Right. I must have had a premonition of disaster even then.' Laughter bubbled momentarily.

Her breath caught in her throat at the sound of his laugh. It was low and amused, and at the same time unnervingly seductive.

'All you could think of at the accident was a story. And now with Paulie you've gone to extraordinary lengths to get another story.' The contempt was back. 'Don't you have any shame?'

Trisha took a breath. 'I can explain. . . .'

'Don't bother.' His tone was harder than she had heard it. 'I couldn't stomach excuses.'

'Please!' She wanted him to think well of her, this man with the long lean body and the gaunt intelligent features. 'If you knew. . . .'

'I know already.' His expression was bleak. 'You paraded as a model and got yourself invited to the party because Gary would be there. Evidently my brother's weakness for a pretty face is common knowledge and you decided to trade on it.'

'Raoul. . . .' she began unhappily, but he did not let her speak.

'Every paper in the country has tried to get an interview with Paulie. All were refused. You were the only one who couldn't take no for an answer.'

'If . . . if I told you this wasn't my idea, I suppose you wouldn't believe me. . . .'

'Correct.'

'Raoul . . . Raoul, I had to do it. My editor insisted.'

'You could have refused.'

'I tried, but I couldn't. I need the money.' Again she stopped. Then, 'You don't believe me, do you?'

Dark eyes flicked her scornfully. 'No, my dear Trisha, I don't. At the accident your compassion had me fooled for a while, then I learned that you were just after a story. And you're after a story again now—a much bigger one this time.'

His manner brought the muscles bunching inside her again, turning her stomach into a tight knot of pain. Why the opinion of this insufferable man should matter to her was something she refused to analyse.

'Whether you believe me is immaterial,' she said, with all the iciness she could muster, 'because I won't be doing the story after all.'

One elegant eyebrow lifted. 'You surprise me.'

She stared at him in confusion. 'You say that as if. . . . Raoul, I'll be leaving first thing tomorrow, as soon as I've spoken to Gary.'

'And that, Trisha Maxwell, is just what you won't do.'

'I don't understand.' Her heart started a sudden painful thudding as taunting eyes lingered on her face. 'I can't stay here, after what's happened. . . .'

He didn't answer. In confusion, she said, 'I can't believe you want me here.'

'Want you?' A short laugh. 'I wish Gary had never set eyes on you!'

'Then I wish you'd explain.'

'Do I have to spell it out?' His gaze was aloof now. 'You came. You're here now.'

'You're thinking of Gary.'

'I'm thinking of Paulie,' Raoul said simply.

'Paulie?'

'Strange as it may seem.' His voice was rough. 'My sister has been through an ordeal, and I just want to see her recover.'

'I can understand that,' Trisha said after a moment. She had the feeling she was on uncertain ground without quite knowing why.

'Since the kidnapping she's been unhappy, insecure, too withdrawn.'

Trisha lifted her eyes to the face inches above hers, registering the stern features, the implacable jaw. 'She doesn't seem withdrawn,' she returned. 'She's been chattering all day.'

Something flickered in the dark eyes. 'She was excited—the novelty of young female company, perhaps. Whatever the reason, Paulie was better today than she's been since we got her back.'

'And you don't want her disillusioned. . . .'

After a moment, the length of which surprised Trisha, Raoul said, 'Right.'

'I'll be gentle.' Through stiff lips she tried a
casual smile, and found it was impossible to be
casual in an atmosphere that was as highly-
charged as if electric currents flowed through it.

'I'll be gentle when I tell her I'm leaving. I'll
think of an excuse.'

There was something unnerving in the way he
was looking at her. He was too near to her. His
eyes were on her lips and her throat, studying her
with an intensity that made her tremble.

'Raoul?' The name emerged shakily.

'You're good at excuses, aren't you?' The tone
was scathing. 'Part of your stock-in-trade, I suppose.'

'Please!' She put out her hands, an instinctive
gesture, as though to ward off an attack of some
kind. The gesture had not been lost on him. His
jaw tightened.

'It seems you haven't understood what I've
been saying,' Raoul said quietly. 'You may not be
leaving at all.'

CHAPTER THREE

HER head jerked back. "What?'

'It's something I've not yet decided.'

The quiet assurance got to her, the self-confident arrogance of a man who was rich and powerful, who all his life had doubtless got whatever he wanted. Anger surged through her, swift and hot. 'You don't decide what I do, Raoul Vareen!'

'That's just what I will do.'

'You don't have the right. . . .' Through a kind of blur she registered the strength of his shoulders and the inflexible line of the jaw; the slow amused curving of his lips, as she'd said, 'You don't have the right. . . .' and then stopped. Perhaps Raoul assumed rights that other men would not. The trembling inside her increased, even as she knew that it was vitally important that she stand up to him. While she still could.

'You gave me the right.' Now there was no mistaking the amusement in his tone, 'When you entered my home under false pretences you gave me the right. It's late, Trisha. Let's stop sparring.'

He was quiet a moment, then he said, 'Paulie likes you. She opened up to you today. You may be good for her.'

Anger was replaced by new confusion. 'I'd have thought it was the one thing you don't want, that

47

she should open up to me.'

'I have been very worried by Paulie's withdrawal. The first days she hardly spoke at all.' The gaunt face became thoughtful with an expression which reached to Trisha's heart. 'Today. . . . Today I saw a change. I hate the idea of this story getting into the papers. But if your being here means that my sister will recover, the consequences may be worth while.'

'You mean . . . you want a companion for Paulie?' Trisha tried to take in what he had said.

His expression changed again as he studied her face. The thoughtfulness was gone now, a hardness had taken its place. 'I told you, I haven't decided.'

Trisha felt suddenly ill. You don't see me as a person at all, Raoul Vareen, she thought. In your eyes I'm just a vehicle that might be of help to you.

Her head lifted, and in the soft light of the table lamp she threw him a burning look. 'I'd have to stay on your terms, I suppose.'

The dark eyes watched her intently. '*If* I decide that you stay—of course.'

'Well, I won't do it!' she said fiercely. 'I shall definitely leave here tomorrow.'

'Perhaps not.' He laughed. 'You're a spunky girl, Trisha Maxwell. I like that.'

The unexpectedness of the words threw her off balance. 'You can't force me to do anything,' she said unsteadily.

'Oh, but I can,' he said, very softly. 'We both know that.'

She knew he was going to kiss her in the moment before he closed the gap that still remained between them. The appalling thing was that she wanted him to kiss her, had wanted it all day. But he was not to know it. His behaviour would become even more arrogant if he did.

'No!' She tried to ward him off, hands pummelling his chest as he drew her against him.

'Yes.' His breath fanned a hot cheek as his arms closed around her. And then his head was descending, and when Trisha twisted her head away his lips found her throat instead. For a moment they lay there, burning against the soft pulsating skin, and then they lifted, never breaking the physical contact, as they moved towards her mouth. So seductive was the trail along her throat that Trisha was quiet in his arms, the crazy thudding of her heart robbing her of all rational thought, causing her to forget the need for escape. This time, when his lips sought hers they met with no resistance.

He kissed her hungrily, as if he'd been wanting this as she had. He began to push her lips apart. Briefly sanity returned, and Trisha kept her mouth tightly closed. She would not give in to him, she *would not*.

And then his hands began to move over her body, exploring the roundness of her shoulders, sliding over her throat where his lips had been, descending to her back once more, tightening his hold so that she could feel the length of him against her. The contact sent a sharp flame of desire shooting through her, and now when his insistent mouth probed at her lips her brief resistance was gone. With a sigh of anguish she opened her mouth to him.

'Nice,' he said, lifting his head for breath, and then he was kissing her again, deeply, hungrily, as if he would never stop.

Mindless, senseless, she was about to wind her arms around his waist when he pushed her away from him. 'I'll see you in the morning.' His voice was rough.

Trisha stared at him, suddenly aghast. For a few crazy minutes she had been lost to all reason, had felt—a feeling that was in her bones, her senses—that he wanted her as much as she wanted him. It was only now, with the break in physical contact, with the dark eyes looking down at her, that she remembered his purpose in kissing her.

'I hate you,' she said as he made for the door.

'You don't.' Raoul turned and she saw that his face was oddly bleak. 'Just as you didn't hate what happened.'

Pointless to deny it—her body had spoken for her. In helpless frustration she let her fingers bite into her palms.

'What do you think Gary will say?' she demanded.

'He won't say anything because he won't know. You won't tell him,' Raoul said softly. 'I'll let you know my decision in the morning, Trisha.'

The door closed behind him. As Trisha turned back to the window where she had been sitting when he arrived, she was trembling violently. The last half hour had shaken her even more than she had realised.

The room had a different feel about it. It was as if something of Raoul still lingered here. There was the suggestion of pipe-smoke and the tanginess of after-shave lotion, a combination that was at once very masculine and disturbingly seductive. Raoul had left the room, but he might as well have been here still.

She could still feel the touch of his body, the depth of his kisses. The recollection of her own responding ardour was uncomfortably vivid. There was a tension in her neck and her spine, so that she wondered if there would be any sleep for her tonight.

Throwing open the window, she took deep breaths of the heady air. It was too dark now to see the garden, but she remembered the glorious profusion of shrubs that grew here, magnolia and frangipani, jasmine and gardenia. At night the scents, always strong, mingled in an exotic profusion that further heightened her maddened senses.

Stop thinking about Raoul, she told herself firmly. Think about Gary. For nothing Raoul can say will make me stay. How do I break the news to Gary tomorrow? And Paulie? What do I tell her? She's been hurt so much already, I don't want to hurt her any further.

The crickets shrilled in the darkness, and from a nearby pool came the occasional croak of a frog. Familiar sounds, country sounds. They should have lulled her, instead they only served to increase her sense of helplessness and isolation.

If only she had never agreed to Carl's suggestion! She had known it was wrong to dazzle Gary for the purpose of coming to Vareen House. But for the pressures on her brother she would have resisted. Had she understood Paulie's insecurity and unhappiness she would have resisted, Jerry's problems notwithstanding.

But it was too late for self-recrimination. She was at Vareen House and now she must face the consequences. One thing was clear—she must leave here. Even Carl could not demand that she stay once he knew that her masquerade had been uncovered.

She went to bed at last, only to lie sleepless. She still did not know what she would say to Gary. Should she tell him she had phoned her brother, that he was ill, that she was needed? More lies. It seemed, Trisha thought unhappily, that once one entered into deceit lies became a web from which it was difficult to extricate oneself.

It was a solution nevertheless, and having decided on it she closed her eyes and tried to sleep. She was tired, so very tired, and she would need all her strength for the obstacles the next day might bring.

It was irritating therefore that an image came into her mind. The lean face was gaunt and mocking, the features as well defined as if she had spent long hours memorising them. She tried to push Raoul from her mind, and found instead that she was pulsating with the memory of the mo-

ments when she had felt more vitally feminine
than ever before in her life.

Considering that Trisha slept only little that
night, she was awake soon after sunrise. Filled
with a sense of lightheadedness—strange that,
after the oppression of the previous night—she
leaped out of bed and ran to the window.

The tropical garden was bathed in the translu-
cence of 'early morning. The jasmine at her
window, the shrub which had smelled so delici-
ously at night, was a mass of tiny white flowers.
A little distance away, its arms outstretched, its
pink flowers a perfection of delicacy, was a frangipani. And in a banana palm—surely the tree must
have grown wild and been preserved by the
Vareens—a brightly-plumed bird emitted hoarse
cries.

Heavens, but this garden was lovely! No matter
that she would be gone from here within a few
hours, she might as well enjoy the loveliness while
she could. Even Raoul could not begrudge her
that. Not that he would know. The house had a
weekend silence which betokened a homeful of
sleeping people.

Trisha had showered and dressed and was on
her way out of the room when she thought of the
swimming-pool. Already it was hot. Soon it would
be unbearable with the humid heat of the tropics.
Now was the perfect time for a swim.

She hesitated only a moment, then she was back
in her room and changing into the rose bikini
she had worn yesterday. In the act of pulling jeans

and shirt over the brief garment, Trisha caught sight of herself in the mirror and smiled wryly at her reflection. The memory of Raoul's disdainful appraisal of her appearance in the bikini was vivid, almost as vivid as the recollection of his hands on her body, of his mouth on hers. She could feel him still. . . .

Stop thinking about Raoul Vareen! she told herself fiercely. You've been thinking about him all night. Dreaming about him. . . .

If the swim achieved nothing else, at least it would clear her head.

The garden was even more beautiful than it had looked from the window. Vareen House was set high on one of the Natal hills not far from Durban, and the lawns were rolling stretches of lush green. There was something joyfully unrestrained about the flower-beds and the shrubs that grew in such profusion. Durban's climate was near-tropical, and in this garden the mood of the tropics was enhanced. The shrubs were great and glorious, their flowers a bright riot of scarlet and orange and yellow. There were many trees, some cultivated and fairly young still, others looking as old as the nearby city itself, with gnarled roots and knotting branches. The banana palm Trisha had seen from her window was not the only wild tree. There were others, more bananas and pawpaws, trees that brought a touch of the primitive to the most beautiful garden Trisha had ever seen.

Emerging from the trees, she came to the swimming-pool. Sun shafted on to the water, so that it looked warm and inviting. With a little cry of pleasure she shed her jeans and shirt.

She was about to dive in, when she saw him. He was at the far side of the pool, where the water was still in shadow, and he was standing quite still watching her. No wonder she had not seen him!

The joy went out of the morning as her eyes held those of Raoul Vareen for what seemed a very long moment. Then she turned her head deliberately and picked up her clothes.

He was at her side before she knew it, a cool hand gripping her ankle. 'What are you doing?'

'Putting on my clothes,' she said icily. She looked pointedly at his hand. 'At least I was.'

In a lithe movement he was out of the pool and standing beside her. 'You were going to swim,' he said.

His closeness was as unsettling as it had been the night before. His body was damp, and hairs clung dark and wet against the bronze sheen of his skin. Her eyes lifted from the virile torso and settled on the hardness of a firm jaw, which seemed the safest place for them to be at that moment.

'I was.'

'And now you've changed your mind.'

'As you see.' It was very hard to maintain the coolness when her senses leaped at the compelling maleness of him.

'Might I ask why?' His tone was lazy.

She shrugged, still keeping her eyes on that very firm jaw. 'I told you, I changed my mind.'

'And that,' he said softly, 'is a lie. You saw

me and took fright.'

'Rubbish!' the word emerged a little too violently.

'Is it rubbish?' Still the same soft voice, seductive and unnerving. 'Look at me, Trisha.'

She stiffened.

'I can't believe my jaw is all that fascinating. Look at my face.'

'Leave me, Raoul. . . .' she said bumpily.

She was turning away—amazing how difficult the act was; almost as if she had been mesmerised to stand in the one spot—when she felt a hand cup her chin, the thumb lying flat against the pulsating skin of her throat. A quiver shot through her, so intense that she could do nothing to conceal it, and at the same time a choked sound emerged from her lips.

'I'm asking you to look at me.'

Jerkily her head came up, and her eyes stared into blue ones so close to her that she could see the flecks of light in the pupils, and each one of the long framing lashes.

'Raoul. . . .'

'You *are* frightened.'

'No!'

'Yes!' The hand that held her did not move, but the thumb began a stroking movement, a slow nerve-tingling movement, down her throat and up again. The breath caught in Trisha's throat.

'Why are you frightened?'

'I . . . I'm not.' She was glad that she had summoned some firmness. 'It's Gary. He . . . he might not like it.'

'Scruples all of a sudden,' Raoul mocked. 'Who'd have guessed it? If it's Gary you're worried about, you can stop. My brother won't wake for another two hours.'

'Paulie,' said Trisha, a little wildly, sensing the battle was lost, not quite knowing what it was she so dreaded. Or did she fear herself and a self-knowledge that was so totally unacceptable that she tried to push it to the farthest reaches of her mind?

'Paulie's probably asleep too. Swim with me, Trisha.'

'No!' She tried to push him from her, and found that the grip on her chin was deceptively firm. 'You can't even stand the sight of me.'

He laughed, the sound even more seductive than anything she had heard thus far. 'I've always enjoyed the sight of a beautiful woman.'

She gaped up at him, and her breath caught once more as she saw warmth lighting eyes that could be so cold. 'You are very beautiful, you know. You're a good reporter—I saw the article you did on the accident—but you could have been a model too.'

He thinks I'm attractive. He really thinks I'm attractive! Expression radiant, Trisha stared at him wordlessly. And then sanity returned, and with it the knowledge that Raoul Vareen was not a man to be underestimated. Female beauty might give him pleasure. It would not cause him to forgive and forget an issue which meant much to him.

The radiance left her face as she looked at him

suspiciously. 'I don't know why you're flattering me. I do know you don't want me here—you made that clear enough. When I've spoken to Gary I'll go.'

'No, Trisha, you won't.'

There was a slight rigidity now in the thumb that still moved on her throat. He was standing so close to her, that she could feel an alertness in the length of his body. She shivered.

'Last night you said. . . . But you couldn't have meant it!'

'I always mean what I say. That's one thing you should remember.'

You said I was beautiful. Did you mean that?

'You can't expect. . . .' she began.

'You talk too much. We'll discuss your future— *after* our swim.'

'If you think I'm going to swim with you, you're quite crazy!' She threw the words at him, her tone unnecessarily high, for she knew it was the one thing she wanted to do. She really *wanted* to swim with Raoul.

'What a stubborn girl you are!' Incredibly he was laughing at her again. 'It seems there's only one language you understand, Trisha.'

No time to escape as the hand that had been on her throat slid to her waist, the other arm curved beneath her knees at the same moment, and then he had lifted her to him.

For a few seconds Trisha lay quite still. When she could think again she would remember to struggle, but now she was aware only of a hard body, damp and strong and intensely male, pressed against her. She could feel him at her back, at her legs, a muscled arm was hard on her breasts, the masculine smell of him filled her nostrils. The feel and smell of him sent a havoc of sensation flooding through her, making her feel dizzy.

It was only when the first rush of sensation had subsided that she tried to move away from him, but in moments she knew that she would have as much chance of succeeding as she would have in freeing herself from the bars of a steel cage. Raoul did not only look strong, he *was* strong.

She could not have said how they got into the water, Raoul still with his arms around her, still holding her against him, but somehow they did. They surfaced, and she blinked water from her eyes, and looked up at him. 'How could you!'

'Easily.' He was grinning down at her, his teeth white and wicked against the gleaming wet tan, and involuntarily she wished he would kiss her.

'Did anyone ever tell you that you look even more beautiful with your hair wet and dragging away from your face?'

'My hair!' She groaned. 'Have you any idea what that hairdo cost me?'

'A fortune, I've no doubt. All in the cause of dazzling my brother. Still, I'm sure a little water won't throw you.'

It wouldn't, of course, for she adored swimming and her hair dried easily in the copper curls that clustered around her head. No need though to tell him that. She looked up at him, pursing her lips in a hard line, only to relax them when she found it impossible to be angry with a pirate's laughing mouth within kissable distance of her own.

Desire was growing inside her, a treacherously erotic feeling that she'd never known with George. She must get away from Raoul, out of his arms. Before she did something she would regret. She had never made the first move with a man, but then she'd never found herself in similar circumstances. Or with such a man. It would be unthinkable for the cool-headed career-minded Trisha to humiliate herself for Raoul's kiss. Yet it was just possible for a girl who felt so absurdly crazy that for perhaps the first time in her life she could not vouch for what she might do.

'Let me go,' she commanded unsteadily. 'I want to swim.'

There was a curious sense of bereavement as his arms left her and her feet touched the bottom of the pool. Swimming was the sport she loved best, as yet she began a determined breast-stroke, she had to give conscious direction to limbs that were languid and weak.

Raoul swam alongside her. He swam crawl, and though she tried not to watch him, she could not help seeing that his movements were rhythmic and without seeming effort. If the time spent in his arms had weakened Trisha, Raoul himself had been in no way affected. For some reason the knowledge was annoying.

Up and down they swam, Raoul always beside her. Up and down, Trisha continuing long after she might normally have stopped, knowing that

when she did stop they would talk, and uncertain
how she would handle it. When she did stop at
last it was because a leg tangled with hers as she
reached the end of the pool and was preparing to
make yet another turn.

For a moment she thought the collision was
accidental. Then, as she stood up, and glanced
into a face that was enigmatically wicked, her
heart thudded against her ribs.

'Raoul, no!'

His only answer was to hook his leg more firmly
between hers. 'You really are a sexy little dish.'
He bent, and before she could do anything to
deflect him his mouth brushed the hollow between her throat and a shoulder. His lips slid
over the smooth wet skin, then pressed against
it.

She was shaking when he lifted his head, and
this time no amount of self-control could hide it.
'You're outrageous!' she accused.

'You'd never call Gary that.'

'G.—Gary?'

'My brother,' he reminded her.

'Gary doesn't behave like this.' She was bewildered.

'You've had no time to know how Gary
behaves. I do know that you'd never call him outrageous.'

She stared at him through eyes that were wide
and confused. 'Are you always so sure of yourself?'

'Only when I have reason to be.' The mobile
lips curved at the corners. 'Having gone out of

your way to charm Gary, you'd hardly insult him.'

The leg between hers was long and muscular, the feel of it so erotic that she did not know how long she could bear it. The contact had brought her whole body into inevitable closeness with his, so that she could see the muscles of his chest rippling beneath the bronze tan, and the pulse that beat at the base of the strong throat. His hands were on her shoulders, their grip light, for it was his leg that kept her near him, yet for all the lightness she could feel each of the long fingers separately against the wet skin of her upper arms.

It was very hard to speak through a mouth that had gone dry. 'You make me sound so ugly!'

'I've said you're beautiful.'

'Like . . . like a prostitute. . . .' she managed unsteadily. 'As if I'm selling myself.'

'Aren't you?' he asked, very gently.

Trisha did not stop to think as she lifted her hand. The slap was sharp and satisfying. Raoul drew in a sharp breath, and then he had forced her hand down, tight between them, the action bringing her even closer to him than before.

'You little hellcat,' he muttered between his teeth. 'Don't you ever do that again!'

'I will if you provoke me,' she countered fiercely. 'You don't scare me, Raoul Vareen!'

He was quiet a moment. Then he laughed, a laugh of real amusement, and it came to Trisha that she did not understand this man at all. 'You're even spunkier than I expected. It will take a strong man to match you, Trisha.'

You could be that man. And how I'd enjoy it.

And then. . . . My God, am I crazy even to think such a thing?

'A man to tame me, don't you mean?' she asked, cursing herself for her breathlessness.

'No man in his senses would tame you, Trisha.' His breath was clean, warm on her throat, fire to her maddened senses. 'Your spirit is part of your charm.'

Keep a clear head. Don't let his flattery get to me. He's shrewd and perceptive, and I'll bet he knows just what his words are doing to me. Like that leg. . . .

'One moment you say such awful things, then you turn nice,' she said slowly.

'And that has you confused?' He sounded oddly satisfied, and Trisha wished she knew why. 'You shouldn't be. You're out for what you can get, we both know that. You've made deliberate and unscrupulous use of your beauty and your charm. The fact remains that you *are* beautiful. And you do have great spirit and charm.' He paused, then said on a new note, 'I feel sorry for Gary.'

She caught her lip between her teeth. 'Why?'

'Because he's not the man to match you.' When he went on he sounded oddly troubled. 'Gary loses his heart to girls easily—but of course you know that. I only hope he doesn't fall in love with you.'

The leg that held hers was doing unimagined things to her senses. Was it possible, Trisha wondered wildly, to want to prolong a mood, while at the same time wishing to end it? She could make no sense of her feelings. But then she had not been able to make sense of them since her first meeting with Raoul Vareen.

'Gary won't fall in love with me,' she stated with a firmness she was far from feeling. 'I won't be around.'

'Yes, my dear, you will.' The voice was cold, ruthless, with an edge of steel.

'No!' She struggled to free herself from him, but the long leg moved quickly, enhancing its hold on her, sending fresh torrents racing through her as she pummelled her fists against a hard chest.

'No, Raoul, no! I've told you a dozen times I'm not staying!'

One big hand captured both of hers easily, the other went to the back of her neck, sliding up beneath the wet curls, the fingers winding through her hair to draw her head backwards. She could not move away from him. Only her eyes were her own now, and then even they seemed not to belong to her, for when she allowed herself a glance into a face no more than six inches away she found that the blue eyes studying her defied her to shift her own eyes away.

'You are staying,' Raoul said very quietly.

'Gary. . . . You said. . . .'

'I do hope my brother won't fall in love with you. But right now it's Paulie I'm concerned about. Paulie needs you.'

'No!' Violently Trisha shook her head. The long muscled hand still held her hair, and the action brought a hairy wrist brushing against her throat. The sensuousness of the touch made her shiver.

Raoul's eyes glittered. Her reactions were not

lost on him, Trisha knew. A man as expert with women as Raoul Vareen, a devil with women, would not be insensitive to the reactions he provoked in one relatively innocent girl. She was powerless to prevent the flush that stained her cheeks.

'Last night you weren't sure,' she said help-lessly.

'This morning I am. Paulie was so much better yesterday. Ten days with her and. . . .'

'Ten days!'

'. . . . she'll be the sister I knew before the kid-napping,' Raoul continued as if she had not regis-tered the interruption.

'You're crazy if you think I'll stay here ten days—or at all!'

'You'll stay.'

'What do you think Carl . . . my boss . . . will say?'

Raoul's hand left her hair, curved round to her cheek, came to rest softly against it in a cool mutual dampness. 'You tell me.'

'He won't stand for it.' It was an effort to force the words from her lips.

'He will when you tell him that the story de-mands a longer stay.' The hand descended, down the front of her throat this time, lingering a moment at its base, trailing further, finding the hollow between her breasts. 'He'll be convinced, Trisha. You make your excuses so convincingly.'

He hates me, Trisha thought as she tried to quell the rush of feeling inside her. The need to have him kiss her was a raw hunger.

'If I refuse?' she asked in a choked tone.

'I can make things very difficult for you.' The words were measured, the voice coldly clinical. 'For your boss, too. I have my means.'

CHAPTER FOUR

TRISHA stared at him, noting again the hard jaw, the strong set of the lips, seeing the eyes that could warm with laughter and which were now an icy metal.

'You're ruthless,' she whispered.

Something flickered in his expression. 'Utterly,' he agreed after a moment. 'You could say we have something in common. We both go after what we want.'

And in that he was right, Trisha supposed, up to a point at least. Only the point was a fine one, and she could not define it for him, not that he would listen if she could. And yes, she thought, he is ruthless. More ruthless even than I understood until now.

'So you want me to be a companion to Paulie.' She lifted her head in a defiant gesture. Let him know that despite everything she still had a will of her own. 'Not that that will be difficult. I like your sister—and your brother.'

'I ought to punish you for the way you said that.'

He moved so quickly that she was caught off her guard as his head swooped down and he took an ear-lobe between his teeth and nibbled on it. He lifted his head again, saw the dazed look in her eyes—each sample of his eroticism left her more shaken than the last—and he laughed, a sound of wicked seduction that was becoming familiar.

'Yes, Trisha, you will be a companion to Paulie,' he said. His tone was as casual as if nothing had happened. And to him the action had in fact meant nothing, Trisha reflected dully. The knowledge hurt.

Yesterday she had decided to abandon all thought of a story. But yesterday circumstances had been different. She had been here of her own will. Now the situation had changed, and with it the need to assert herself.

'On my conditions,' she said.

He moved, shifting his position deliberately. The water ebbed about them, and Trisha felt a fresh tingling as Raoul's leg and thigh became imprinted upon a new part of her leg.

'I don't think so,' he drawled.

His tone, even more than his words, made his meaning unmistakable. Heat flooded her face. Throwing back her head, she said bitterly, 'You're the most arrogant man I ever met! You know damn well that I was talking about the story. I will be writing it, Raoul.'

'I know,' he agreed. 'Just two things I insist on—I read the copy; and don't trade on intimacy to get personal details.'

A business bargain, sealed and signed in its own way.

'Let me go now,' Trisha ordered.

'In a moment.' The suggestive drawl again. Trisha stiffened. She knew by now that the tone betokened danger.

'We've said everything,' she said quickly.

'Not quite.'

Caught by something in his tone, she looked up at him. She did not know that her mouth was soft and vulnerable, and that her eyes were troubled and confused.

'I'm going to enjoy seeing you around,' Raoul whispered.

'Are you always so contradictory?' she asked in a choked voice.

His lips were curved in a smile that was half mocking, half amused. 'I wish you'd never intruded here, Trisha. That hasn't changed. But you have, and you *are* beautiful, and I do enjoy beautiful women.'

As his arms tightened around her she knew he was going to kiss her. She wanted it; it was a wanting that had increased moment by moment with the intoxicating closeness. She also knew it was important to keep away from him. Would there always be this conflict? she wondered.

She twisted her neck sideways, but Raoul easily thwarted the token protest, his mouth sliding on to her throat, brushing sensuously up to the averted face, letting his tongue rest at the corner of a trembling lip. The eroticism of the touch sent a shudder through Trisha, so that she turned to him in unthinking surrender.

'That's better,' said a husky voice, and then his arms were folding her even closer to him, and a hand reached for the back of her throat to pull her head back.

Trisha parted her lips for one last protest, but

as his mouth crushed down on hers, the words—
words that had not yet been formulated in a mind
half-crazed with wanting—were drowned. His
kiss was deep, hungry, demanding response, and
receiving it. His hands had moved their position,
one sliding to her waist, the other to her hips,
arching her against him. She could feel her breasts
against his chest. Through the thin fabric of the
bikini she could feel him almost as if she wore
nothing at all.

The hand that had been on her waist came forward, slid beneath her bra, cupped a breast and
began to caress the nipple, and she could feel that
the nipple became hard in his fingers.

Raoul was a tall man, much taller than she was,
but now their heads were on a level. Through her
mounting desire Trisha was aware of the thrill of
being weightless in the water. Her feet were
against his calves, and she could feel both his legs,
the shape of his thighs an unforgettable imprint
against her own.

Her hands went to his shoulders, probing the
bone and muscle, then they hooked themselves
around his neck. Later she would wonder with
horror what he might have made of her behaviour.
Now there was just the need to learn the shape
and texture of his body, to be close to him. They
had paused for breath when a cry rang through
the trees.

'Raoul! Raoul, are you there?'

His reactions were lightning-swift. In less than
a second he had released Trisha's arms and
pushed her from him. By the time Paulie emerged

through the trees he was on the other side of the pool.

'Swimming?' called the young girl. And then, stopping short, 'Trisha's here too.'

'Such a perfect morning,' Trisha's heart was pounding so hard that she marvelled the other two could not hear it. Raoul seemed unaffected by what had just happened. The easy smile he gave his sister indicated that.

'Coming in, lazybones?' he asked.

The girl took a step backwards, and the look of haunted fear came into her eyes. '. . . . No.'

Yesterday Paulie had not swum either, Trisha remembered. Did water have some special connotation? she wondered now. Or had Paulie merely become so fearful and introverted that she shunned all experiences. The latter, she guessed.

'The water is super.' As Trisha lifted a slender arm and splashed a few drops at Paulie's feet, she was smiling. There, Raoul Vareen, don't for one moment think your lovemaking meant anything out of the ordinary to me either! 'You'll love it, Paulie,' she cried.

A mixture of expressions crossed Paulie's face, temptation and fear, a little of each. 'Perhaps later,' she demurred.

'Later we'll swim again. Come in now.'

Paulie smiled suddenly. 'Okay. It does look good.'

'You'll get changed, then?'

'Yes. . . . Yes, I will. And I'll bring Gary back with me.'

Paulie ran away through the trees towards the

house, her movements infused with sudden eagerness. Watching her, Trisha was unaware of the man who had come up behind her. When two hands gripped her shoulders she tensed.

'Good girl,' he murmured.

'For God's sake, Raoul!'

'Go on in that vein and you'll earn your story.'

She pivoted in the hands that once more were doing such alarming things to her senses. 'I was just being friendly.'

His thumbs moved upward, sliding towards her ears. 'Go on just the way you are.'

Already she could feel the new stirrings of desire. 'Let go of me,' she said shakily. 'Don't you know you disgust me?'

'I know that you're a warm-blooded woman.'

'Raoul!'

'Raoul,' he echoed mockingly. 'Don't try the injured maiden act on me, Trisha. You enjoyed every minute of our lovemaking. You'd have let me go further if Paulie hadn't happened to come along.'

She shook her head blindly from one side to the other. 'No! I wouldn't have.'

'Yes. We both know it.' The exploring thumbs found another path, down into the hollow between breasts that were still hard with excitement. He gave a low laugh. 'Your body gives its own invitation.'

'I'm cold,' she whispered on a sob. 'Let me get out.'

'I was hardly about to go on making love to you with Paulie and Gary due to burst in on us any moment. But just remember one thing, Trisha,' the dark head bent and his mouth claimed hers in a kiss that was brief yet possessive, 'I meant it when I said I'd enjoy your stay here.'

Paulie said, 'Gary, I'm so glad you persuaded Trisha to remain here longer.'

'Not half as glad as I am.' Gary's voice was warm as he put an arm around Trisha's shoulders.

Trisha shot a glance at Raoul, a long lean figure sitting in apparently lazy silence. Nothing in his pose indicated that he had manipulated the situation, that Gary's coaxing had resulted from Raoul's own very subtle suggestion. Only by the merest flicker of an eyebrow did he register Trisha's indignation and discomfort. And then she saw that his eyes were lit with enigmatic amusement. Deliberately she moved her head.

'How long can you stay?' she heard Paulie asking.

'I'm not sure.' Trisha kept her head averted.

'We'll certainly make the most of it.' This from Gary as his fingers closed intimately on the soft flesh of her upper arm.

Raoul spoke for the first time. 'We'll certainly do that.'

Caught as much by his voice as by his words, Trisha swung round. Only to regret the action, for the eyes that watched her gleamed more intensely than before. Raoul's statement had been meant only for herself, Trisha knew. A little wildly she looked at Gary, then across to Paulie.

Are you both blind? she screamed at them silently. Don't you see what's happening? Judging by their expressions it seemed that they did not.

Shrugging Gary's hand away, she stood up. 'I have to make a phone call.' In her own ears her voice sounded brittle. More gently she went on, 'I have to speak to my boss.'

'Your boss?' Paulie was confused.

Another unwilling glance at Raoul. 'Yes. I'm just assuming I can stay longer. I ... I have to make sure there are no assignments waiting.'

Without another word she was walking away from them. It was true that she had to speak to Carl Samson—not that his answer was in doubt. What was more important was to get away from the Vareens, from the eagerness of Paulie and Gary which shamed her, from the amused contempt of Raoul which had her enraged.

'Miss Maxwell?' Carl Samson was astonished to hear from her. 'Where are you?'

'Vareen House.'

'Is it all right to talk?'

'Yes ... yes, it's okay.'

'How goes it?'

'Fine. The Vareens want me to stay longer.'

'You're making progress?'

'Yes. But it can't be hurried.' Clutching the receiver tightly in her fingers, Trisha was finding it difficult to talk. Just minutes ago Paulie had been almost pathetically pleased that she was staying. How would the girl take the truth if she learned it?

'Mr Samson ... Mr Samson, I hate what I'm doing.'

'Baby, baby. . . .' Indulgence crept into the abrasive tone. 'You're a newspaper-woman. This is part of the job.'

And if I quit the job? If I decide that, after all, this is just not my scene?

'Remember the raise,' he said, as if he sensed her thoughts. 'Your efforts won't go un-rewarded.'

Jerry, you are my very dear brother, but why don't you learn to stand on your own feet? Do you know what you're expecting when you demand more and more money?

'I know the rewards,' she said in a subdued tone.

'Don't sound so sad. Vareen House must be quite a place. What's it like there, Miss Maxwell?'

It's special, very special. The most beautiful home I know. And its owner is unique. Raoul Vareen is the most dynamic man I ever met. He's. . . .

No! How *could* she let herself voice such thoughts, even silently. Raoul Vareen was arrogant and supercilious, and she would be happy to leave here, never to see him again.

'It's very beautiful,' she said quietly.

'Terrific! Perhaps you can do a feature on it next, get photos.'

'I have to go. . . .'

'Keep in touch, Miss Maxwell. Oh, one last thing—some guy's been phoning. George?'

George must be wondering what had happened

to her. He'd been out of town when she'd begun this assignment, and she'd not been able to let him know that she would be away. When was the last time she had thought about George? Trisha wondered guiltily. Hardly at all since the morning she had met Raoul Vareen at the scene of the accident. Not once in the time that she had been at Vareen House.

She dialled his number. At the sound of his voice she made an effort to relax limbs that were unnaturally tense. George was a fine man, solid and dependable. Stuffy . . . The irreverent adjective Sally had once used to describe him came involuntarily to mind. No, he was *not* stuffy, though that perhaps was how he would seem to a stranger. Trisha, who knew him so well, understood that he was a good man, that she was lucky to have him for a friend.

'Honey, are you all right?' He sounded concerned.

'Fine. Just fine.'

George could be more than a friend if that was what she wanted. Twice he had asked her to marry him, and though he had been disappointed at her hesitation he had made it clear that he would ask her again. What was keeping her back? she wondered, as she heard him tell of his efforts to track her down. George was an architect with a lucrative practice. He was patient, kind, definitely not arrogant. In fact, he had all the personal qualities a good husband should have. He had everything . . . everything except the ability to set the blood singing in her veins.

Trisha held the phone a little away from her ear and looked at it aghast. Did she have to have fireworks exploding in her nerve-stream before she could make up her mind to get married? Surely not—she was twenty-three after all, and knew that that kind of romance was not realistic. Fireworks indeed! Till just recently she had not even known that a man could stir her to wildness.

But she knew now! There had been fireworks with Raoul, fireworks exploding in her veins and in her heart and in her brain, filling all her being with delicious excitement. Somehow it did not help to tell herself that Raoul Vareen was possessed of all the qualities she most detested. The fact remained that in his arms she had known what it was to be a woman. It was a knowledge which would never leave her. Worse, Trisha knew that she might forever find herself comparing every man she met with Raoul, and find each one lacking. Just as soon as she got back to Durban she would tell George she would marry him, she decided.

'I really wish you hadn't run off without telling me,' George was saying. He sounded exasperated, even sulky. And stuffy. Oh God, please not stuffy!

Damn you, Raoul Vareen, isn't it enough that you've done crazy things to my body, now you're even manipulating my mind!

'I would have told you, George.' It took surprising effort to keep her tone patient. 'It happened rather suddenly. And you weren't around.'

'I get the feeling you haven't told me the whole truth.'

He was right, of course. Silly of her to wish he'd change the subject. Perhaps she'd feel different if he sounded less stuffy. No, she *could not* think stuffiness again!

'George, it's difficult for me to talk right now,' she said.

'Be careful of those Vareens. I don't trust them.'

'George, I'm on a job,' she told him.

'I know.' His tone was measured, calm. 'And I do understand. I'm just asking you to be careful.'

Don't be so understanding! Demand that I leave here. Charge in and force me to leave. As Raoul would do if the girl he loved were involved in something like this. . . .

Across the hallway a movement caught her eye. Raoul had come into the house. He was leaning against a doorway, one long tanned leg stretched lazily before him as he watched her.

The nerve of the man! Trisha treated him to her most scathing glare. The look was meant to discomfit him, but he must have been amused for his lips curved in a smile. Hiding her anger, Trisha spoke into the phone, 'George, I'm glad you understand. Listen, dear, I really must go.'

'Trisha . . . Trisha, I miss you.'

This was the George she had known for more than a year, the man who would make a good husband. Perhaps she had only imagined the previous sulkiness, for now his voice was warm once more.

'I miss you too,' she said, and hoped it was only in her ears that the words sounded flat. 'Goodbye, George.'

Raoul was still leaning against the doorway as she made to go past him to the garden. The lazy tone stopped her. 'Well, Trisha Maxwell. All is settled?'

Abruptly she pivoted, 'Do you always listen to telephone conversations?'

'Only when they interest me.' The enigmatic dark gaze held hers.

'You can stop spying on me,' she snapped tautly. 'We have an agreement.'

'I hope we do.' No mistaking the warning in the quietly spoken statement. Trisha dropped her eyes from a look she could not sustain. There was ruthlessness in this man, and he would not be slow to use it if the occasion warranted. A shiver ran through her.

'Trisha. . . .'

'Leave me alone, Raoul,' she got out through clenched teeth. 'Just leave me alone!'

Gary would be waiting for her on the verandah, but Trisha took a different path. She had to be alone a few minutes before she could indulge once more in laughing small-talk.

Earlier this morning she had noticed a secluded piece of garden on her way to the pool, and she went that way now. Gratefully she sank down on a soft patch of grass, and let the peacefulness of the setting drain the tension from her. Azaleas fringed the grass, the flowers lovely in a profusion of pink and white and mauve. A little farther back, tall and vivid against the cloudless sky, was a flame tree, its branches a riot of scarlet so vivid that the colour looked almost gaudy against the gentler hues of the azaleas.

Closing her eyes, Trisha listened to the sounds of the garden. There was the ceaseless droning of the bees, the repetitive call of a bird. You don't need me, Paulie, she thought. Not really. You have two adoring brothers and this lovely garden. However bad your ordeal was, and I know you did suffer, you could get over it without my help.

At a rustling sound she opened her eyes. A monkey was perched on a branch not more than five feet away, another was on the ground. Two pairs of eyes were fixed on her, jewel-bright and intent. Suddenly, as if on cue, they leaped upwards, swinging from one branch to another, swooping, diving, playing.

Trisha laughed, the sound loud and merry. And then, as if the uncaring merriment of the monkeys brought home the helplessness of her situation, she buried her face in her hands.

'A dryad,' remarked a laughing voice.

She had not heard him approach. Keeping her hands over her face, she waited for the racing heartbeats to subside.

'Trisha, you're not crying?'

Surely that was not concern in his tone? Arrogance was the quality she expected in Raoul Vareen. She did not like it, but she was learning to accept it. Concern, when it was applied to herself, might well be more than she could handle.

'Go away,' she muttered through her fingers.

'Look at me.'

With her hands still in front of her face, she shook her head.

'Yes.' A hand went to her neck burning on the vulnerable skin left bare by her bending head. A moan of pleasure rose inside her, but she stifled it, and instead she made herself sit very still.

'I'm not an ogre,' Raoul said softly.

'Then why do you behave like one?' She dropped her hands as she spoke. 'I'm not crying, Raoul. It's all right—you can leave me.'

'You're beginning to sound like a record. Leave me, Raoul. Go away. . . . Do you know how many times you've said that?' His voice dropped to a seductive softness. 'Perhaps I don't want to leave you.'

Heart hammering painfully, Trisha turned her head and looked up into eyes that were dark and alert. He had manipulated her into a situation she detested, had shown her little but contempt until now. There was no sense in the fact that she longed to cover his hand with hers and keep it on her neck for ever.

'You followed me,' she said at length.

The dark head nodded.

'Why?'

'I'd have thought it was obvious.' The hand slid from her throat to her shoulders, going beneath the loose cheesecloth blouse. She felt his fingers, as if each had a life of its own.

'What did your boss have to say?'

'He's satisfied,' she managed through parched lips.

'Did he offer you a raise?'

The wandering fingers had moved forward, and
were now edging slowly, sensuously, towards the
top of a breast. Trisha felt as strung up as a piano
wire. It was all she could do to retain sufficient
control not to let Raoul see quite how much he
was affecting her. The effort of conducting a conversation at the same time required a superhuman
effort.

He was still standing beside her. Wetting her
lips with her tongue, she turned her head once
more and shot him a deliberately flirtatious look.
'As a matter of fact he did,' she lied.

She heard a hiss of insucked breath, and then
he had stepped closer against her. She tried to
move away, but found it was impossible. His
hands encircled the front of her body, his legs
were a wall that held her captive from behind.

'Good,' he said softly. 'See that you work for
it.'

His thighs were tight against her back now. She
could feel them imprinted upon her, felt as if she
knew the long shape of them, the hardness of each
muscle. The contact triggered a response in her
that started at her toes and shafted up to the very
tip of her spine. She tried to close her mind
against the sheer sexual impact of the man, but
found she could not. It was as if Raoul invaded
every part of her being. And that was the worst of
it, she thought despairingly. Sexual attraction
alone could be coped with, however difficult it
might be, but Raoul's attraction was made up of
something else. There was something about the

man that seemed to intrude into her mind, her heart, and her soul.

Don't do this to me, she begged silently. To you a woman has only one function—especially a woman whom you so obviously despise. My feelings are different. For me to feel quite so strongly about a man there must be caring, loving. . . .

No! Not love. Never love. Not with you, Raoul Vareen. There can only be unhappiness with a man like you.

'I'll be working,' she said shakily.

'I don't mean the story. Though I'm sure you'll do your darnedest with that. I'm talking of Paulie.'

'I mean to help her.' It was unnerving to talk with Raoul's legs pressed against her. It was as if he enveloped her on all sides with his body.

How would it be to be married to this man? To lie beside him each night in a shared double bed. To make love, fully, unlike this promise of intimacy that tantalised and frustrated.

'I will help her,' Trisha said shakily. 'I want to be alone now, if you don't mind, Raoul.'

'How did your boy-friend take the news?' Raoul questioned, just as if he had not heard her plea.

'You were listening,' she accused. 'Why ask?'

'Does he mind that you're staying in another man's house?'

'Of course not. He . . . he knows I'm just working.'

A throaty laugh was the sole response, as the muscled thighs exerted a deliberate and increased pressure.

Trisha's heart did a painful double beat, then

slowed just a little. 'George trusts me,' she defended shakily.

'With full reason, I've no doubt.' A husky seductiveness. 'You said you missed him.' A hand moved downward, found a space beneath the lacy bra, began a slow exploration of a firm round breast. 'Does George have reason to think you might not be missing him as much as you said?'

'N-None at all.'

'No reason for dull George to think he might not be able to trust you?' The hand found the nipple, stroked it, played with it. In moments it had hardened beneath his touch. 'No reason for him to think you'd be unaroused by someone else?'

'I'm not aroused! And George is not dull.'

'Now, Trisha, there are two lies you don't get away with.' Again the low laugh, openly seductive. 'Your lips frame the words so easily—any lie so it seems—but your body tells the truth.'

'You've no right to do this to me,' she accused.

'Talking of rights again?' The hand was still on her breast, and now the other arm was circling her body, folding beneath her diaphragm, drawing her even more closely, if that were possible, against the hard wall of his thighs. 'You've done exactly what you want until now, I do likewise.'

'Raoul, you. . . .' The words stopped in her throat as she felt an earlobe caught between strong teeth.

'You want to tell me how terrible I am?' he queried in a tone of quiet amusement, letting go of the lobe. 'Don't, Trisha. You're enjoying this as much as I am.'

'I'm—not!'

'Yes, you are.' His lips nuzzled a path down her throat, lingering at the base, then moving up again. Then he asked, 'Tell me, does your George arouse you?'

I've never felt a thing with George. Oh, his kisses were pleasant enough, but I never experienced this fire that sets my body alight. I never knew I could feel quite so vital and feminine, so heedless of consequences.

'All the time,' she managed brightly.

'Then how could you bear to leave him? Even for just a few days?'

'My job,' she said desperately.

'If you were mine,' he said on an odd note, 'I wouldn't let you get away from me even for a few days. No job could be that important.'

But I'm not yours, and thank goodness for that. It would be sheer hell to be shackled to an arrogant, demanding egoist. I wouldn't want it for the world.

But I do want it, whispered another voice, small yet insistent. And it wouldn't be hell at all. It would be a kind of heaven, because the expectations would be a mutual thing, and there would be a wonderful loving that would make all else seem natural and right.

'How close are you to this George character?' Raoul asked.

The demands of her body, coupled with Raoul's amused contempt, brought out the devil in her. 'Very close,' said Trisha, answering the question she had never been able to bring herself to answer with George. 'We're going to be married.'

Did she only imagine the sudden tightening in the legs pressing against her? 'It seems to me that a girl with as much spirit as you have would have much more sense than to enter into a gutless marriage,' Raoul said in a voice she had not heard before.

If only he would stand facing her, so that she could see his eyes when he talked. The way he held her, from behind, was not only unnervingly sensuous, it was also frustrating.

'Why do you call it a gutless marriage?' she countered. 'You don't know George at all.'

'I don't have to.' His hands were moving again, stirring her awakened senses to a frenzy. 'I heard the way you spoke to him, and you sounded like a demurely affectionate acquaintance. I feel the way you respond to me—there's nothing demure about you, Trisha Maxwell, no matter what your George might like to think. I don't give your marriage a chance.'

'I don't care what you give. . . .' Trisha began on a note of frustration, only to stop at a sound in the trees.

'Trisha! Raoul!' Gary's voice was high with anger. 'What the hell's going on here?'

'What should be going on?' Raoul countered easily, as Trisha stared aghast into the flushed young face.

'You and Trisha. You've been making love to her!'

'Don't jump to conclusions.' There was authority in Raoul's voice, even now, when he'd been surprised in a compromising situation.

'You're so close to her ... and your hand, on her neck. ...' For the first time Gary sounded uncertain.

'I just saved your Trisha from an insect bite.' Raoul laughed shortly as he stepped away from her. 'Don't look so stricken, Gary.'

'Well, as long as that was all.' Gary stared after his brother who was now making his way through the trees, his gait as smooth as if nothing had happened. He turned back to Trisha. 'I still don't understand how the two of you came to be here together.'

'I made some phone calls.' Trisha's breathing had settled somewhat, and it was easier to speak. 'Afterwards I thought I'd sit here a few minutes. It's so ... so beautiful. Raoul found me here.' She ventured a glance into eyes that still held the vestiges of doubt. 'Raoul was right—don't make too much of it, Gary.'

'Well, okay,' he shrugged.

She got to her feet. 'Were you looking for me?'

'Yes. The Lattimer girls want us to come over.'

'Oh?'

'Yvonne, and her sister Salina. Paulie would like to go.' His expression lightened. Trisha thought how likeable he was, more likeable surely than Raoul. He was standing very near to her, and she wondered why his closeness did nothing to affect a heartbeat that responded so violently to his brother. 'It's the first time she's felt like going anywhere since ... since the kidnapping,' he said. 'I just came to tell you.'

CHAPTER FIVE

HAZELDENE, the home of the Lattimer sisters, could not compare with Vareen House for size and beauty, but it was an impressive estate all the same. Seated in a reclining chair, with a cold ginger ale at her side, Trisha looked around her and reflected that she was catching a glimpse of a gracious living style she had encountered for the first time a few days earlier. The garden was carefully cultivated, and beneath the lawn the orchards fell away—acre upon acre of fruit-trees.

The visit had begun under strain. Yvonne Lattimer, whom Trisha took to be no more than nineteen, had been flushed and ill at ease. Though she had made an attempt to be friendly to Trisha, the small pretty face was unhappy. Frequently she glanced at Gary, and now and then she laughed, but the laughter sounded forced. Once, when Yvonne sat alone and seemed to think herself unobserved, her eyes glinted with tears.

Trisha felt a surge of sympathy for the girl. A wave of female instinct told her that she was in love with Gary. There was something infinitely likeable about the slim young girl with the sweet fresh looks. If rumour were true, Gary's inclination drifted from one glamorous girl to another, but so far none of his attachments had been lasting. At Hazeldene lived the proverbial girl-next-door. Yvonne would make a perfect wife for Gary; Trisha marvelled that Gary did not see it.

Yvonne left the lawn, only to come back minutes later with a puppy in her arms. 'Mitzi's last-born,' she announced to the visitors, but her eyes were on Gary.

'You're kidding!' Gary's exclamation was eager. And then he was on his feet and holding his arms out to the puppy.

Within minutes Gary and Yvonne were playing on the lawn, laughing as the puppy ran and yapped at their heels. The earlier strain dissolved like rain puddles in the sun. How young in his ways Gary was, Trisha thought. Young and eager and playful. And so right with this sweet girl who loved him.

She glanced at Raoul, who was lying on the grass, one leg bent, the other stretched out before him. An eyebrow lifted in response, making words unnecessary. If only you'd never come into my brother's life, his expression seemed to say. It came to Trisha that Raoul would welcome a union between Gary and Yvonne.

She wondered why Raoul had never married. It could not be for lack of opportunity—such was his appeal that any woman would leap at the chance of sharing his life. *Almost* any woman, Trisha corrected herself angrily. Even if a miracle were to happen and he were to grovel at her feet, she herself would not wish to be shackled to a man of such arrogance.

'Raoul!' At the sound of the husky voice she turned. 'Raoul,' Salina Lattimer called again, 'you haven't seen the new stallion.'

'Behaving himself, is he?'

'He's gorgeous. Come see, Raoul.'

Without a word he got to his feet. Trisha saw that he was smiling as he fell into step beside the voluptuous blonde to whom she had taken a dislike almost at first sight. Salina was talking as they talked away, and Raoul, his dark head inclined towards hers, laughed in amusement. Trisha was unprepared for the pain that knifed her chest as she watched.

It was an effort to respond to Paulie's chatter, and she was relieved when the girl joined Gary and Yvonne's antics, for the pain in her chest had not gone. Jealousy was an emotion she had never experienced, but self-honesty made her admit that she was experiencing it now. It was particularly galling that the emotion should be connected with Raoul.

Blindly Trisha turned her head away from the strolling couple. It seemed that with Raoul she had entered a whole new world of feelings. This was so only because he was the most devastatingly attractive man she had ever met, she told herself desperately. It was a sheerly physical thing, a question of chemistry. That there could be anything deeper she could under no circumstances accept.

Jealousy was awful, she decided, thinking she could hardly feel worse. But she did feel worse when Raoul and Salina returned from the stables some twenty minutes later and Salina said, 'Darling, you will be here early on Wednesday,

won't you? We have that date with Phil and Ann,
and I promised Ann we'd be on time for once.'
The words were spoken with such easy familiarity
that it was clear a relationship existed between
these two, and that it was of long standing. That
the relationship was more than just neighbourly
was emphasised by the sultry intimacy in Salina's
manner, the possessiveness of the manicured fingers resting on Raoul's bare arm.

For one more reason Trisha wished she had
resisted Raoul's insistence that she stay on at
Vareen House.

Paulie was still romping on the lawn. For a
while she played with the others, her laughter
mingling with theirs. Meeting Raoul's eyes,
Trisha wondered what he made of his sister's
merriment. On the surface she seemed contented
enough. No stranger, seeing her now, would guess
at the ordeal she had so recently endured. Was
Raoul making too much of things, Trisha
wondered, when he insisted that she stay to help
Paulie forget the kidnapping so that she could pick
up the threads of a normal life once more?

Raoul's eyes held hers steadily. The sun made
it difficult to read them, but she sensed that they
were intent. It seemed as if he had read her
thoughts—as he did so often—and was silently
telling her that he disagreed.

Perhaps, after all, he was right. Paulie was
laughing now, her manner as carefree as Gary's.
Yet there were times when despair was in her face,
when she seemed to withdraw to some inner core
of her being where none could follow. Perhaps

Paulie was indeed a soul in torment.

'May I see the stallion?' Paulie asked suddenly, tiring of the game and looking across the lawn at Salina.

'I'll take you,' said Raoul, before Salina could speak. 'Let's leave Trisha and Salina to get to know each other. Salina is interested in fashion, so there must be lots you can tell her.' The last remark was addressed to Trisha, and the wicked winking of one eye was something that only she could see.

Somehow she managed to quell the flush that rose in her cheeks. With a smile she said, 'I adore talking about fashion.'

But Salina, it seemed, was less interested in fabrics and colours than in the topic of Raoul. 'Isn't he a hunk of a man?' she said when he was out of earshot.

'He's interesting,' Trisha responded noncommittally.

'Interesting! My dear, he's more than that.' There was an odd inflection in the husky voice. 'Of course, I'm hardly unprejudiced.'

'Oh?' Trisha felt a quiver of apprehension.

'There's been an understanding—old-fashioned word that, but I don't know another—between myself and Raoul for years.'

'In that case you're right, your views may be prejudiced;' Trisha smiled and hoped that Salina did not catch the strain beneath her deliberate lightness.

The smile hid a returning pain. Salina's words had been nothing less than a warning—keep away from Raoul, he's mine.

A puzzling warning indeed. The Lattimer sisters knew that Trisha was at Vareen House as Gary's guest: it was this fact that had made Yvonne so unhappy. Yet Gary had not been mentioned. Why not? Had an exchange of looks made Salina suspect that a relationship existed between Trisha and Raoul? Had Trisha betrayed her interest by an unguarded facial expression? Raoul had certainly done nothing to arouse the girl's suspicions; his behaviour towards Trisha had been cool and remote.

'Staying long with the Vareens?' the golden-haired girl wanted to know.

'A while.'

'For a busy model life at Vareen House must seem very boring.'

'Not at all.'

'It will.'

Was that venom in the well-modulated tone? Looking up, Trisha saw a pair of hostile eyes fixed on her face. Salina's unjustified viciousness brought out the worst in her. 'I'm finding life with the Vareens extremely enjoyable,' she said sweetly.

The sweetness hid her tension. With nails curled into the palms of her hands, she wondered what had caused Salina's viciousness. All the cards were surely stacked firmly on the other girl's side. Apart from her well-bred beauty, she must have all the requirements required of a mistress of a big estate. Life at Hazeldene would quite naturally have provided the training Raoul's future wife would need. Above all, it seemed Salina and Raoul were already as good as engaged.

Did Raoul love this girl with the perfect body and the icy eyes? Perhaps he did. If he did not, it would not matter, Trisha decided crossly. Both parties would get out of the marriage what they wanted. Raoul would have a beautiful wife and an impeccable hostess. Salina would have undoubted status and the many benefits that went with it. If Raoul paid attention to other women—and the lovemaking Trisha had experienced since coming here as Gary's guest suggested he would do so— then perhaps this was something Salina was prepared to overlook.

Such a marriage would never do for herself, Trisha knew. She would only marry a man whom she loved, and she would not be able to condone his games with other women. The thought crossed her mind that she would never fall in love if she compared every man she met with Raoul.

And that is absurd! she told herself angrily, trying to push the thought from her conscious-ness. Raoul is no different from other men. He doesn't mean a thing to me, when I go home I'll never have to see him again.

Nevertheless it was impossible to stop her heart from leaping as a voice enquired, 'Time for a swim?'

He was standing above her, tall and straight and handsome, every lithe inch of the copper-tanned body proclaiming his virile masculinity.

Eyes that could be as cold as steel were blue

and warm and amused. You know what we were discussing, Trisha thought wonderingly, I don't know how, but you do.

Salina was right—he was a hunk of a man. Except that he was more than that, she decided as she got gladly to her feet. He was special, no matter how much she tried to tell herself otherwise. He could be ruthless yes, but he was also warm and human and caring, and the woman who married him would be the luckiest girl in the world. That girl could never be Trisha herself, but it was a shame that she should be Salina. Raoul Vareen deserved better than the disdainful ice-maiden.

'We're always swimming,' she said lightly.

'You've been swimming together?' Salina put in, before Raoul could speak, and her voice was pitched higher than Trisha had heard it.

'The most pleasant pastime right now,' Raoul answered easily, and his gaze skimmed Trisha's face as he talked, as if he made a silent comment on Salina's hostility. 'Durban is always hot, but this last week it's been torrid.'

'Yes, well. . . .' Salina shot a furious look at Trisha, but did not go on with the sentence.

In the water they were joined by Gary and Paulie and Yvonne. Paulie's cheeks were rosy from the game with the puppy, and Trisha was glad to see that the unhappiness had been chased from Yvonne's eyes. She was laughing at something Gary had said, the sound clear and merry. Yvonne was fun, Trisha thought, and so nice. If only Gary would realise that she was no longer

the coltish neighbour he had evidently known for
as long as he could remember.

They had been in the pool a few minutes when
Trisha felt two hands enfolding her waist from
behind, and then she was being pulled down-
wards. As her feet found a foothold on calves that
were rock-hard, an arm bent quickly backward to
encircle Raoul's neck. The ducking was short.
One moment they were below the surface of the
water, her body pulled tight and hard against
Raoul, his mouth making a quick path along one
shoulder and up her throat. The next they had
surfaced, Trisha laughing and choking, her arm
still around Raoul's neck as if she needed the support.

Her laughter ended abruptly as she registered
the silence in the pool. The other four had stopped
swimming, and were watching Raoul and herself
with expressions that ranged from surprise to
anger. And then Gary was advancing upon them,
thrashing the water fiercely with his arms. Trisha
drew a breath as she pushed herself from Raoul.

'How dare you!' Gary shouted, treading water
beside them. 'I told you to leave Trisha alone!'

'Take it easy,' Raoul cautioned. 'It was just a
game.'

'Game nothing! You've been after Trisha since
the moment you saw her. She's *my* girl.'

'Raoul's right,' Trisha intervened. 'It was just
a game, nothing more.'

It *was* more, and you know it, Raoul Vareen.
And why I'm defending you heaven alone knows.

She looked from the firm-jawed implacable face

Say Hello to Yesterday

Holly Weston had done it all alone.

She had raised her small son and worked her way up to features writer for a major newspaper. Still the bitterness of the the past seven years lingered.

She had been very young when she married Nick Falconer—but old enough to lose her heart completely when he left. Despite her success in her new life, her old one haunted her.

But it was over and done with—until an assignment in Greece brought her face to face with Nick, and all she was trying to forget. . . .

Time of the Temptress

The game must be played his way!

Rebellion against a cushioned, controlled life had landed Eve Tarrant in Africa. Now only the tough mercenary Wade O'Mara stood between her and possible death in the wild, revolution-torn jungle.

But the real danger was Wode himself—he had made Eve aware of herself as a woman.

"I saved your neck, so you feel you owe me something," Wade said. "But you don't owe me a thing, Eve. Get away from me." She knew she could make him lose his head if she tried. But that wouldn't solve anything. . . .

Your Romantic Adventure Starts Here.

Born Out of Love

It had to be coincidence!

Charlotte stared at the man through a mist of confusion. It was Logan. An older Logan, of course, but unmistakably the man who had ravaged her emotions and then abandoned her all those years ago.

She ought to feel angry. She ought to feel resentful and cheated. Instead, she was apprehensive—terrified at the complications he could create.

"We are not through, Charlotte," he told her flatly. "I sometimes think we haven't even begun."

Man's World

Kate was finished with love for good.

Kate's new boss, features editor Eliot Holman, might have devastating charms—but Kate couldn't care less, even if it was obvious that he was interested in her.

Everyone, including Eliot, thought Kate was grieving over the loss of her husband, Toby. She kept it a carefully guarded secret just how cruelly Toby had treated her and how terrified she was of trusting men again.

But Eliot refused to leave her alone, which only served to infuriate her. He was no different from any other man. . . or was he?

These FOUR free Harlequin Presents novels allow you to enter the world of romance, love and desire. As a member of the Harlequin Home Subscription Plan, you can continue to experience all the moods of love. You'll be inspired by moments so real...so moving...you won't want them to end. So start your own Harlequin Presents adventure by returning the reply card below. <u>DO IT TODAY!</u>

to the one that was flushed and vulnerable. 'It *was* a game, Gary,' she pleaded.

'I don't know. . . .'

'Don't be an idiot, Gary.' Raoul's tone was clipped. 'You're making too much of what happened. Remember we're guests here and don't ruin the day.'

Gary's colour was still high. He had the truculent look of one who was spoiling for a fight. Despite the fact that he would stand no chance against Raoul who would be able to stop the altercation with a single well-aimed blow.

'Gary,' Raoul warned softly.

Slowly, reluctantly, the younger man backed away, and Trisha drew a sigh of relief. Without a look at Raoul she swam away. The air rang with the sound of splashing as everyone began to swim once more. An ugly moment had been averted, but Trisha had the feeling it would be some time before it was forgotten.

It was almost midnight when she heard the knock at her door. As she went to answer it, it came to her that she had been expecting Raoul. In the circumstances she might have done better to keep on shirt and jeans instead of donning a transparent pink nightie.

He came in quickly, closing the door soundlessly behind him. For a moment there was silence in the room as he towered above her, the dark shade of his trousers and rolltop sweater emphasising the animal-like quality that seemed always to be a part of him. Trisha found her gaze drawn from the proud thrust of throat to lips that were firm yet sensuous, and upwards again to eyes that were set arrogantly beneath thickly winging brows. At times there had been understanding in Raoul's face, even a particular kind of gentleness that some very masculine men possess. Now there was just a relentless unbending. Trisha shivered, frightened all at once, yet at the same time very excited.

'You knew I'd come?' he demanded without preamble.

'I thought you might,' she admitted.

'And yet you chose to wear this.' His eyes savaged the nightie, and she trembled as she realised that he could see through the thin fabric to the curves and planes of her body.

'It's midnight,' she protested. 'I was almost asleep.'

'Eve,' he said, his tone changing to a seductive taunt. 'Your name should have been Eve, you play her so well. The eternal woman, teasing, flirtatious. You have all the provocative qualities of your sex, Trisha, those that drive men to madness. Do you also have the finer qualities?'

The trembling had increased. 'You didn't come here to discuss my womanhood.' Her voice was as low and as controlled as she could make it.

'No, though we can get to that later.' His eyes held hers before descending once more to the slim curvaceousness beneath the diaphanous garment.

'Get to the point!' Trisha hissed.

'About the incident in the pool. It shouldn't have happened.'

Incredulously Trisha looked up into a face that was a chiselled mask of strength and power. 'You've come to apologise?'

'Any apology would not be directed to you. You asked for what happened.'

'No!'

'You did—by inveigling yourself into this house. And with your provocative clothes and your sexy beautiful body. Yes, Trisha, I deeply regret what happened and my part in it. But my regrets are for Gary and for Paulie. I don't like needless friction in my family.'

'You can't blame me . . .' She caught her lip beneath her teeth and stared up at him. 'I didn't lead you on.'

'You lead me on with that irresistible loveliness of yours.' He took a step closer, his hand reaching out to cup her throat, his fingers sliding to the base of her head to bury themselves in the soft hair. 'My God, Trisha,' his voice was husky, 'you're so beautiful!'

Happiness leaped within her, like a small caged bird fluttering to get out. She did not resist as he drew her to him, moulding her slight form to his hard one, his hands moving slowly, sensuously, over her back to her waist, then lower to her hips. As his mouth found hers her lips parted willingly, and flames were ignited up and down her spine with the movement of his hands and mouth, and desire was a wild stirring within her.

There was no rational thought now, only a heady welter of sensation. She was arching her body to his when he pushed her from him.

'What. . . . Why. . . .' She stared at him, dazed.

'Why did I stop kissing you?' His tone was fierce.

Trisha nodded. Was she not experienced enough for him? Did the beautiful Salina give him more satisfaction than she did?

'Because if I don't stop now I'd have to make love to you—all the way, Trisha. Don't you know it's what I want?'

As she wanted it. The revelation was frightening, yet exhilarating.

'Then why. . . .'

She heard him draw a breath as he seized her shoulders. There was nothing lover-like in his touch now, 'I came to talk to you.'

'I see,' she said dully.

'I think Gary means to propose to you.'

She was still so shaken by his embrace that she found it hard to think clearly. 'Propose?' she asked, bewildered.

'Marriage. He wants to marry you.'

There was a long moment of silence. In the dim light of the bedside lamp Trisha saw Raoul's face change, the jaw tightening, the lips curving in a look that she was getting to know too well. 'Marriage,' he said again, his voice laced with contempt. 'Though if he knew that you'd just as soon consent to be his mistress he might be more hesitant to commit himself.'

'You're a bastard!' Trisha hurled the words at him through a flame of anger.

'Perhaps I am. But I'm not under discussion right now. What will you say to him, Trisha?'

Don't you know that I could never marry Gary? That he means nothing to me? That I see him only as a very sweet kind young man?

The anger was still so raw, that she took pleasure in provoking him. 'That's something that would be between Gary and myself, surely.'

The grip on her shoulders increased, the fingers biting into the soft flesh. 'I have to know.'

'Let go of me!'

'When you've answered me.'

'You're hurting me.'

The pressure of the fingers lessened. Whatever else he might be, Trisha thought through her anger, Raoul Vareen was not a person who would inflict physical hurt deliberately.

'Trisha!' No mistaking his frustration. This tall strong man was not accustomed to being thwarted by anybody, least of all by an unco-operative girl who by all logic should be intimidated by him.

She lifted her chin, and the look she slanted him was both provoking and defiant. 'I still say it's none of your business, but. . . . As a matter of fact, I don't know what I would say.'

'I find that hard to believe. A girl with your kind of self-will doesn't have difficulty with decisions. What about George?'

'What about him?'

'You said you might marry him.'

'And you told me such a marriage is doomed,' she reminded him.

'I still think so.'

'But now you wish I'd marry dull George— your adjective, Raoul—after all.'

Something came and went in his face, an odd expression which Trisha could not define. She was not sure why she felt a sudden racing in her veins.

His tone suddenly quiet, Raoul said, 'I just don't want you to marry Gary.'

'If I do?'

'I would do my very best to put a stop to it,' he said evenly.

'You don't think I'm good enough for your brother?' Trisha asked on a small wave of pain.

'Good, bad . . . don't talk in clichés. I don't want you to marry him, let's leave it at that.'

'No. You're so adamant about this, Raoul. I have to know why.'

'For one thing, you're not suited to each other. Gary's image of you is that of a lovely innocent girl, sweet, pliable, happy to give up your career for him.'

'Like Yvonne,' Trisha suggested.

'Like Yvonne,' Raoul agreed. 'Now there would be the right wife for my young brother.'

As her sister would be for himself. Raoul and Salina. A comfortable understanding made secure by years of proximity and moving in the same circles. The pain Trisha had felt before stabbed at her now. As if she'd lost something, she thought. But could one lose a thing one had never possessed in the first place?

'The other reason,' she prompted through dry lips, forcing herself to talk in the hope that the pain would lessen.

In the small silence that followed her question

Trisha was too overwrought to register the movement in Raoul's throat and jaw. At length he said, 'I couldn't bear to have you married to my brother.'

She stared at him. 'Isn't that what we've been talking about?'

'For a very clever female you're slow on the uptake.' His hands returned to her shoulders. Now the fierce matter-of-factness was gone from the touch, and in its place was a familiar sensuousness. '*I* don't want you for Gary. I'm thinking of myself now, Trisha.'

She forced herself to stand very still as long fingers slid over her soft upper arms, then back to shoulders that were bare save for the thin straps of the nightie. Under no circumstances would she betray the series of tremors that ran through her.

'I may be very foolish. . . .' she began.

'Or perhaps you're even cleverer than I thought.' His voice was softly seductive as his hands moved further, his thumbs lingering on the little pulse in the hollow of her throat—the one part of her she could not control—then further, to trail a burning path towards her ears.

'Raoul. . . .'

'Raoul, make love to me, is that what you're saying?'

'No!'

'It had the sound of it, but no matter. I want to make love to you.' His tone had become even more seductive. 'And that's it, Trisha. I couldn't stand to see you with my brother. If you were married to Gary I'd want to make love to you each time we met.'

He was attracted to her! Elation thundered through her. At the same time a warning sounded in some cautious part of her mind—be careful, this man is shrewder than all the other men you know put together.

'You're crazy,' she said.

For answer he pulled her against him, abrupt and hard. His body was against hers, the long length of it. She could feel the tautness of muscled thighs, the hardness of narrow hips, the steel of his arms and the pounding of his heart. This time she was unable to conceal the shudder of longing that swept through her.

'If I'm crazy, you are too,' he said, and she knew the reaction had not escaped him. He laughed, the sound husky and low and fire to maddened senses. 'Crazy and beautiful and very desirable.'

'You really mean that?' The words were out before she could stop them.

'Can't you tell?' She was held so tightly against him that she could not tilt her head to see his face. His throat vibrated against her cheek as he spoke, and the quickened beat of his heart seemed to keep pace with her own.

'Now you know why you can't marry Gary,' he said after a moment. 'I'd hate to make love to my brother's wife.'

'I wouldn't want you to anyway.'

'You're kidding if you think that. Don't you know it?' He bent, and his tongue drew a roughly sensual path along her throat at the same time as his hands slid to her waist and moulded the shape of her beneath his fingers. Trisha was powerless to prevent a moan of pleasure.

'You do know it. We both do.' He had lifted his head and his tone was oddly troubled. After a moment he went on more quietly, 'God knows I've done things I haven't been proud of, but I wouldn't stoop to making love to my brother's wife. If you marry Gary you'll be torturing us both.'

No point in denial; they'd passed that point. And her words would only be made ridiculous by the treacherous responses of her body.

'Pity I didn't follow up our first meeting,' Raoul said, putting her a little way from him so that she could look into his face.

'Why didn't you?'

'You know that too.' He had not released her entirely, and now a hand trailed a teasing path in the hollow between her breasts, the fragile night-dress offering no resistance.

'I was a reporter,' Trisha said shakily.

'Right.' He paused. Then, 'Gary is too young for you. He could no more keep you satisfied than could dull George. But you and I . . . we'd have made a great pair.'

Trisha swallowed, hardly able to take in what she was hearing. Raoul Vareen saying these words! There had been many shocks in the past few days, many surprises, but what she was hearing now was possibly the biggest surprise of all.

'You mean *you*'d have married me?' she asked incredulously.

There was a subtle change in the hands that held her. 'Marriage? Who said anything about marriage?'

Trisha flinched at an amusement that was more devastating than anything that had gone before. 'Why, you. . . .'

'I said we'd have made a great pair—sexually, and in other ways too.'

'You thought I'd be your mistress? That I'd have an affair with you?'

'What else?' Still the cool amusement.

There was no way Trisha could tell him how far her thoughts had winged in the space of a few moments, of the intense happiness she had experienced. Instead she said hotly, 'You're an even bigger bastard than I thought!'

'Oh, come, Trisha.' He had changed position, and now the glow of the light cast a sheen on his face. 'You'll be telling me next that you're a virgin.'

She bit her lip. 'Would you believe me?'

'Wouldn't I be very gullible if I did?' He was watching her intently. 'A girl who's prepared to go to the lengths you did, who very expertly makes a play for a man—without him even being aware of the fact, mind you—and then goes to his home—I'd be a fool to believe that girl was a virgin.'

'Put that way it sounds horribly incriminating, I know.' She looked at him, unaware that her eyes were huge pools of distress. 'But, Raoul, it's true.'

He was silent a long moment. His face was aloof

as he studied the slight feminine figure. Trisha did not know that he took in every detail of her appearance, from lips that trembled and a pulse that beat too quickly at the base of her throat to the skimpiness of the thin nightdress, and that he thought how vulnerable she seemed.

When he spoke his tone was abrupt. 'I can understand why Gary fell for you. He never did stand a chance.'

'You don't believe me then. . . .'

His eyes became hooded, enigmatic. 'That's immaterial. I still say we'd get on well together.'

'I would never be your mistress!'

'Wouldn't you?' he drawled.

And then she was in his arms, and he was covering her face with kisses, his lips teasing and tantalising, drawing an aching response from her body. Heedless of the dictates of her mind, she was kissing him back, receiving pleasure and giving it. As his hands moved to cup her breasts her hands began an exploration of their own, glorying in the feel of cool skin and hard muscle.

He raised his head suddenly and looked down at her, their eyes meeting in a long timeless moment. And then his arms tightened around her once more, and he was lifting her from the ground. Panic welled as Trisha saw that they were moving towards the bed, there was the flashing knowledge that her world was rushing towards a climax and that nothing would ever be quite the same again.

Think quickly! Do I want this thing to happen? No . . . it's against everything I believe in. And

yes, yes, yes, I want it! It's crazy, but I do . . .
with Raoul, and here in this room. Nevertheless I
must not. . . .

The decision was taken from her as a scream
rang through the silent house. And then another.
Just inches from the bed, Raoul paused in mid-
step.

'Paulie!' he exclaimed as he dropped Trisha
to the floor. 'She's having a nightmare.'

CHAPTER SIX

HE was out of the room in seconds, Trisha following him. Paulie lay in her bed, racked in a spasm of agony, tears streaming from closed eyes, lips contorted. She was unaware of their presence as another scream emerged from her throat.

'Paulie! Paulie dear, you're dreaming.' Raoul was by her side, lifting her head from the pillow and supporting her neck with one hand. 'Paulie, wake up!'

The girl in the bed took a gasping breath and then her lashes fluttered open. Her eyes were dazed with horror and her face was wet.

'The wolf,' she whispered faintly.

'Paulie, there is no wolf.'

'Yes, yes! It was howling ... coming to get me.'

'No. Look where you are, dear. This is your bedroom. And look, here's Trisha.'

'Trisha ... yes. . . .' Eyes in which the terror was subsiding focused a moment on Trisha. Then she went on, 'The wolf, Raoul—it was there. I know it was!'

Paulie would never get back to sleep while she remained in this state. It took Trisha just a few minutes to fetch a glass of milk from the kitchen and a cool cloth from the bathroom. When she came back into the room she saw that Raoul was

stroking the tangle of hair from the damp forehead. His movements were tender, she saw, incredibly tender for such a very strong man. She
was swept with a wave of longing to feel his ten-
derness—if only once—for herself.

His eyes caught hers as she came to the bed
and began to dry Paulie's face. A brief glance, but
in it there was approval. Absurdly, Trisha's heart
leaped.

And then he was talking to Paulie, soothing her
in a voice Trisha had never heard him use.

'It's always the same dream, Raoul,' Paulie
insisted, she sounded quietly desperate. 'Always
the wolf ... always there, at the mouth of the
cave ... howling, its jaws snapping. ...'

Raoul will interrupt her, Trisha thought. He
will tell her again that there is no wolf, that there
never could have been, because there are no
wolves in Africa. But he allowed her to continue.

'How could they do it to me, Raoul? Did they
have no pity?'

'No, dear, it seems they didn't.'

When Trisha had finished wiping Paulie's face
she held out the glass to her. 'No.' Paulie waved
it away, but Trisha said, 'Yes, just a little,' and
like a child, obediently, Paulie took a few sips.

'Why, Raoul, why?' she asked again when she'd
handed the glass back to Trisha.

'They were ruthless. Some people are. They
used your fear to get you to write the notes.'

'The notes ... yes. They dictated every word.
Only the writing was mine.'

Here was the story Carl wanted. It was the story

no other reporter had been able to get. Paulie, young and lovely and vulnerable, in the grip of merciless men. A very different Paulie this was from the young girl who had romped on the lawn with Yvonne's puppy. This was a girl who was tortured by dreadful memories, unable to put her ordeal into perspective and then relegate it into the background of her life. Oh yes, there was much here that Carl would relish, including the brother—a tycoon esteemed in the business world—who comforted Paulie when she screamed.

Had Raoul forgotten why she was at Vareen House? If he remembered, he gave no indication. Easy enough to ask her to leave Paulie's room now that the worst of the crisis had passed, but he did not do so. Perhaps she should leave them alone together, nevertheless.

Yet, as if she was mesmerised to one spot, Trisha was unable to move. Watching Raoul with his sister she found it hard to reconcile the hard arrogant man who had made passionate love to her not more than ten minutes ago, with the gentle person she saw now. A lump formed in her throat. She would remember these moments, just as she would remember the fierce longings Raoul had aroused in her. She *wanted* to remember them, though there would be unhappiness in doing so.

'You must think me stupid. . . .'

She gave a start as she realised that Paulie had addressed her. 'Stupid? Oh no,' she said. 'You've been through a dreadful ordeal.'

Turning, Raoul beckoned to her to come closer

to the bed. 'I think Trisha understands,' he said.

'It's the same dream every time—the wolf, the howling. Oh, I know there are no wolves in Africa, but it was there. I'll never forget it!'

The only light in the room came from the lamp beside the bed. It cast a small golden pool on the thick rug, enveloping them all with its glow. There was a sense of intimacy here, Trisha thought, as if they were three people who belonged together. The next thought came unbidden—how wonderful it would be if her part in this group could be assured always, and of right.

'One day you'll forget.' Raoul was saying to Paulie. 'But first. . . .'

He did not finish the sentence as the door was flung open and footsteps sounded in the room. Pivoting, Trisha saw Gary, a flushed and rumpled Gary in mismatched pyjamas.

'What's going on here?' he demanded.

'Paulie . . . a nightmare,' Raoul explained.

'The usual, Sis? The wolf?'

'Yes. Gary, it was awful!'

'I know.' He turned, and for the first time he seemed to take in Trisha's presence in the room, and the fact that she and Raoul stood close together. 'Trisha! Why are *you* here?'

'They came when I screamed,' Paulie supplied before Trisha could speak.

'Together?' It was an accusation. As Gary looked from her to Raoul, Trisha saw that his face was wild and angry. 'What were you doing together? You were making love to her, Raoul! I've told you to keep your filthy hands off Trisha!'

Feeling a little sick, Trisha stared at Gary. She felt helpless, vulnerable, she did not know what to say.

'Don't jump to conclusions,' Raoul said calmly, and Trisha caught the warning look he flicked her. This was not the right moment for the truth. 'We both heard Paulie scream and came to help. That's all there is to it.'

'You mean . . . you weren't together?' Gary was slightly mollified. Trisha should have been relieved, yet she could only feel disappointment that the lovely intimacy there had been moments earlier had been destroyed.

'Think about it.' Again Raoul evaded the question. He was handling the situation in the only way possible, Trisha supposed. A confrontation now would be disastrous.

'I'm sorry.' Yet despite the apology, Gary still did not look happy. 'It's just. . . . Trisha in this nightdress, and you seeing her. . . .'

Cool dark eyes ran impassively over Trisha's figure. 'I've seen women in less. Let's just concern ourselves with Paulie, shall we?'

Trisha was grateful that he had turned the attention away from herself. But later, alone in her room once more, she shifted restlessly between the sheets.

She was frightened. Raoul had twisted the truth to avert a scene. But Gary's jealousy was growing. It was not impossible that the time would come when he might walk in on a love-scene between Raoul and herself, and she shuddered at the thought of his reaction.

Waiting her opportunity, Trisha phoned Jerry the next morning. Her brother was happy to hear from her, naïvely eager to learn if she was enjoying herself. Only at mention of money did his voice grow anxious.

'I must have the money.' His voice was brittle.

'Can't you speak to Saunders? Get him to accept monthly payments?' Though Jerry's fear alarmed her, Trisha tried to keep her voice calm as she made the suggestion.

'I have, but he won't agree.'

'Jerry. . . .' she began.

'I must have it. Sis, you promised!'

'I know.' The hand that held the phone was white-knuckled. 'But it . . . it's not that easy. . . .'

'Why not?' Jerry demanded. Not for the first time Trisha wondered if firmer handling on her part when Jerry was younger would have resulted in her brother behaving more responsibly. 'Your boss said he'd make this worth your while.'

'That's true.'

'And the Vareens are loaded. Everyone knows that. They'd give you a loan if you asked for it. You must be great pals by now.'

Trisha's toes curled at the thought of asking Raoul Vareen for a loan. Asking him for any favour at all.

'I've taken enough advantage of these people as it is,' she said tightly.

Something in her tone must have got through to her brother, for when he said, 'I know, and I do understand,' he sounded genuinely sorry.

'Well then. . . . Jerry, can't you get out of this

mess on your own?'

'No. If I don't do what they ask they'll make things tough for me.' His voice sank to a whisper of despair. 'They might even kill me!'

'Stop being so dramatic,' she said firmly, concealing her own fear.

'It's true. Trisha, I'm sorry, honestly I am, and it won't happen again—ever—but I need that money. This Vareen story will be really something. None of the other papers have it. And Mr Samson did say he'd pay you.'

'All right, Jerry.' The helplessness within her seemed to start at her feet and fill her whole being. 'I'll help you. But this is the last time—the very last time, Jerry.'

'Okay.' She was about to lower the receiver, when he asked, 'What made you phone?'

'You know the reason.'

'You don't want to do the story?'

'No.'

'Why not?'

She stared down at the phone as if she could see right through it to her brother. Strangely, the face that formed in the shiny blackness was not Jerry's at all—it belonged to Raoul. She shuddered.

'Because it isn't right,' she said faintly. 'I'm here under false pretences.'

'You were prepared for that. Sis, what happened to change your mind?'

'I got to know Paulie,' Trisha said very simply. 'I like her, Jerry. She's not the spoilt rich girl you might imagine. She's sweet and young and very shaken after what she's been through. She has a right to her privacy.'

'There's something else.' Her brother spoke with surprising perception.

'Yes.' Trisha took a deep breath. 'There is something else. I have to go now, Jerry.'

'Sis. . . .'

'Goodbye.'

Slowly she walked away from the telephone. She could not have walked any faster, for her legs were very weak and she felt quite drained. Had she been as naïve as her brother, she wondered, to think that the phone-call might be the answer to the problem that had kept her awake most of the night?

The situation was becoming intolerable. She did not want to write about Paulie. She had made up her mind on that point very soon after arriving at Vareen House. Her views had not changed. If anything, as her affection for the pale unhappy girl increased, there was a growing distaste in knowing that she was learning more and more about a story to which she had no right.

Yet it seemed she might have no choice. Jerry's despair had been genuine. Knowing the company he kept, it was possible that threats had indeed been made to his life. Somehow she had to find a way of giving her brother the money he needed.

As for the 'something else' that Jerry had perceived. . . . She had not wanted to tell him about the men at Vareen House: Gary, transparent and friendly, yet suspicious of his brother's manner towards Trisha, getting a little more jealous every day, and Raoul, dark and tall and arrogant, a man who could make her angrier than she had ever been; who could stir her to heights she had never dreamed possible.

Just the thought of Raoul was enough to cause a dizzy buzzing in her head. So much so that she did not see Gary as he came running up the steps, and she fell as they collided.

'Did I hurt you?' He was concerned as he helped her up.

'No.' She laughed up at him. 'I should have watched where I went.'

'Where's Raoul?'

The laughter died in Trisha's eyes. 'How would I know?'

'You seem to be with him so much. . . .' The words trailed away. 'I'm sorry, I guess I'm jealous.'

'You shouldn't be,' she told him. 'Raoul doesn't even like me.'

'Then I'm making too much of things?'

'I think you are,' she said gently.

'You're so lovely.' Gary's voice was suddenly husky as he took a step closer. 'We've not had enough time alone together.'

'Gary. . . .'

'Tonight, at the party, we'll dance,' he told her.

She looked up at him. 'Party?'

'Raoul's birthday, didn't you know? Paulie suddenly thought it would be nice to have a party for him.'

He stepped closer still, and an arm closed around her shoulder. I feel nothing, Trisha thought, nothing at all. If this was Raoul's arm I'd be warm with excitement.

'We'll be together,' Gary said. 'Let's go swimming this morning, Trisha, just you and me. We'll give Paulie and Raoul a skip.'

'Sounds fun.' She managed to keep her voice light as the hand on her shoulder tightened. 'This party . . . will there by any guests?'

'The Lattimer girls.' Gary's tone altered a fraction. 'I wouldn't be surprised if Salina is hoping to make her engagement with Raoul public tonight.'

'They are unofficially engaged, then?' Trisha asked very carefully, glad that Gary's vantage point did not allow him to register the sudden paling of her face.

'Of course, didn't you know?' There was an eager recklessness in Gary's tone. 'So you see, Trisha, there'd be no point in your falling for Raoul.'

'I've no intention of falling for your brother,' she said with deliberate firmness. 'It's murder in the sun—let's go for that swim.'

The recklessness in Gary's manner persisted in the pool. It made Trisha a little uneasy, so that while they frolicked in the water she was never entirely relaxed. It was as if he was trying too hard to be playful and unconcerned. Though she herself felt anything but playful, Trisha tried to fall in with Gary's mood. It seemed important that she humour him.

Once, when a long shadow fell over the sparkling water, her head lifted. Raoul stood by the side of the pool. He was long and taut in well-cut white trousers and a navy shirt, a tautness which extended to his facial expression. Trisha felt herself grow hot beneath his scrutiny. Gary was holding her, one arm beneath her knees. He had been about to toss her into the water. Now, caught by her sudden rigidity, he looked up too, and she heard his small intake of breath. Then he bent and kissed her deliberately on the lips. Turning her head just a little, Trisha saw Raoul's lips tighten with the contempt she was growing to know so well, then he turned and walked away.

'I couldn't stand to see you with my brother.' The words he had spoken last night came back to Trisha now. She hardly noticed that Gary had dropped his arms as she stared after the lithe departing figure.

'Why did you do that?' she whispered.

'I wanted to kiss you.'

Caught by his tone, she turned to him. His colour was high, his lips tight. 'You wanted to prove something to Raoul.'

Gary hesitated a moment, then he said, 'Perhaps I did. It's time my older brother understood that what's mine is mine.'

Trisha stared up at him. 'I'm not yours, Gary.'

'You're here with me,' he countered defiantly.

'But I don't belong to you. I don't belong to anybody.'

Not to you, Gary. Or to George, with his

paternalistic disapproval of my behaviour, or to
Jerry who thinks he can lean on me for ever instead of taking responsibility for his own life. I
don't belong to Raoul. Raoul, who thinks he has
the right to subject me to his lovemaking or his
contempt just as the mood takes him.

Least of all do I belong to Raoul!

'Trisha. . . .' Gary was looking down at her, and
now the defiance was gone from his face, and his
eyes were troubled. 'Trisha, don't be angry.'

'I'm not angry.' She tried to make her voice
casual. 'But I don't belong to you, Gary. You have
to understand that.'

'Does that mean that you and Raoul . . .?'

'It just means that we're friends, you and I.
That I'm here as your friend, Gary, nothing
more.'

Did he understand that she had evaded the
question? That she had answered him with a half-
truth? It was true that Raoul felt nothing for her.
The fact that he had made love to her—and very
passionately at that—did not mean a thing. To
Raoul Vareen lovemaking was a purely physical
thing; his emotions were in no way involved. But
Trisha's own emotions were a different matter
altogether. To Gary she could assert that Raoul
meant nothing to her. With herself she had to be
more honest.

'Trisha. . . .' Gary was still holding her, and
now she felt his arms tightening, drawing her
closer against him. She managed to turn her head
as she saw his descending.

'I want to kiss you, Trisha.'

'No. . . .'

Unable to reach her averted mouth, his lips touched a cheek instead. 'This is for real, Trisha, nothing to do with Raoul.'

There was such feeling in his tone that she turned again to look at him. 'Gary. . . .' she began.

'You don't belong to me, not yet. But, Trisha, I think I'm beginning to. . . .'

She put a finger quickly to his lips. 'Don't say it, Gary. Keep it light—please!'

The handsome young face darkened, then visibly relaxed. 'You're different from other girls. But I'll play it your way if that's what you want.'

'Thank you.' Anger and fear made a knot of pain in the pit of her stomach. How would Gary react when he found out why she was here, and that Raoul had in fact made love to her? Would he be very hurt? For as Raoul had warned, this very nice young man was falling in love with her— at least so he thought. There was some consolation in the knowledge that his previous loves had turned out to be infatuations and that it did not take Gary Vareen long to console a broken heart.

'Let's swim,' she suggested, smiling up at him.

The eyes that met hers were blue and intense, the arms that held her were rigid. Trisha felt herself tensing. She'd hoped Gary would release her, and wondered how she'd cope if he did not.

'Let's swim,' she suggested again, lightly. 'Afterwards you can tell me about the party.'

Gary stared at her a few moments longer, then

he released her with an abruptness that seemed
alien to his character. 'All right.' His tone was
hard. 'We *will* play it your way, Trisha.'

Trisha took care in dressing for the party. She
had not wanted the expensive clothes Carl had
insisted on providing, yet as she studied her image
in the mirror she felt a perverse satisfaction in the
knowledge that she was looking her best—a feeling, she knew, that had something to do with the
fact that Salina Lattimer would be here tonight.

The dress Trisha had chosen was as deceptively
simple as only an outrageously expensive dress
can be. The lovely garment made the most of her
slender figure, enhancing curves she had not
known she possessed, and at the same time giving
her a look of seductive elegance. The neckline was
beautifully cut, revealing something of honey-
coloured shoulders and the swell of high breasts.
All the dress needed was one simple adornment.

Thoughtfully Trisha fingered the emerald pendant left to her by her grandmother. She had
packed it on impulse, not really believing that she
would have occasion to wear it, yet including it in
a gesture of defiance as being the one lovely thing
that was her own. It was a piece she wore only
seldom, for with her more casual garb it was
usually inappropriate.

Even now she wondered if she should wear it.
And then a picture of Salina Lattimer came to
mind once more. That girl would be decked out
in her best.

Trisha clasped the pendant around her neck

and saw that the emerald set off the sea-green dress to perfection.

Any thoughts that she might have overdressed were dispelled when the Lattimer sisters arrived. Yvonne looked even prettier than the first time Trisha had met her. Shining chestnut hair curled softly at the top of her shoulders and a halter-necked dress flattered her small figure. Trisha wondered when Gary's eyes would open to Yvonne's blossoming loveliness.

Salina looked stunning in a dress of deep scarlet, with her golden hair swept backward in a coil to emphasise the perfection of her features. Trisha wondered if it was only jealousy that made her think of a huntress on the prowl.

The girls had come bearing presents, a home-made cake from Yvonne, a tie-pin from Salina. There had been presents from Paulie and Gary too. Only Trisha had nothing, and for the first time she wondered if she should have asked Gary to drive her into town.

Raoul was at the stereo changing a record when she took the opportunity to talk to him. 'Seems I'm the only one with no gift.' She smiled up at him, her glance teasing from beneath her long lashes.

He straightened and looked down at her, his gaze moving slowly and deliberately over her figure before coming to rest on her face. 'You could give me the best gift of all,' he said, his voice seductively caressing, his meaning clear.

Silly that her heart should miss a beat, for by now she should be immune to his outrageousness.

'Don't you ever stop?' she asked low-toned.

'Not when I want something.'

He was closer to her than she'd realised, so close that she could smell the clean tang of an after-shave lotion that was becoming too familiar. He was dressed in casual clothes, well-fitting brown cords with a matching shirt open to just above the waist. Trisha thought she had never been more aware of a virile maleness so strong that it threatened to overpower her. With an effort she took a step away.

'Where are you going?' he asked softly.

'G-Gary must be wondering where I am.' The breath skittered in her throat as she felt his fingers at her chin. 'Raoul. . . .'

'Will I get the gift I want?' he asked, as if he had not heard the protest.

Yes! Her whole being seemed directed at the answer. Frightened by the violence of her responses, Trisha tried to take another step back, only to find that his grip was stronger than she'd imagined, imprisoning her beside him.

'Let me go,' she said shakily.

'You haven't answered me.'

'You know the answer.'

'Meaning yes.'

'Meaning no!'

'You want it, Trisha.' Still the seductive quality that wrought such havoc with her senses. 'And I want it. I mean to have you in my bed, Trisha.'

From behind them came the sounds of the party. Gary's laugh rang out, then Yvonne's softer response. The stereo was in the corner of the long room, away from the table where a buffet had been laid out. Had they not been missed? Trisha wondered wildly. Raoul must be very sure of himself to behave this way when Gary's jealousy could erupt at any moment.

His fingers left her chin as he threaded both hands through her hair, framing her face. 'What's making you play the prim virgin I wonder?' he said.

'I am a virgin.' Her voice was unsteady. 'I've told you that before. I'm not playing at primness. And when I do decide to sleep with someone it won't be with you, Raoul Vareen!'

She knew she'd made a mistake the moment the statement was out. A muscle moved in his jaw, and then the hands about her head tightened, and the pressure of his bent arms was pulling her to him. They were so close now that Trisha could feel the warmth of him through the thin fabric of her dress. She closed her eyes, feeling suddenly dizzy.

He was bending to her, when an abrasive voice said, 'I'm not interrupting anything, I hope?'

Trisha's eyes snapped open just as Raoul, sounding not at all discomfited, said, 'A birthday kiss, Salina.'

'Well, if that's all. . . .' Though the other girl pretended to be appeased, the gaze that rested on Trisha was suspicious. 'I'd have thought Gary would mind.'

'Mind his brother receiving a birthday kiss?' Trisha fell in with Raoul's game with a lightness which surprised her. 'I don't believe it!'

Involuntarily her eyes went to Raoul. His face was without expression, but in his eyes was a gleam. Trisha could not have said quite why she felt a moment of intense satisfaction.

She was moving away when Salina said, 'That can't be an emerald.'

She doesn't like me, Trisha thought, and she said, 'Why not?'

'Too big. A fake if ever I saw one.'

Trisha had no time to answer as long fingers lifted the pendant from its resting-place just above her breasts.

There was utter silence as Raoul studied the stone. Even Salina seemed suspended in a tense moment of waiting. Finishing his scrutiny, he did not let the emerald fall back into place. Instead he put it there gently, his fingertips lingering on the soft swell with a lightness that made Trisha tremble.

'No fake,' he announced. 'I know something about stones, and this one's a beauty.'

'It must be worth a fortune,' Salina breathed. And then, with a return of her abrasiveness, 'Where did you get it?'

Trisha stared at her, registering the tone, but not understanding its meaning. 'Why do you ask?'

'Well—a model,' Salina shrugged. 'There must be men in your life. Besides, Gary. . . .'

As the outrageousness of the remark made its impact, anger brought a flush to Trisha's cheeks. 'My grandmother would have given you a tongue-scalding for that one,' she said hotly. 'She loved this pendant.'

Again Raoul's eyes gleamed. No mistaking his approval this time. Trisha wondered if he would say something to his fiancée by way of reproof, but he did not. Instead he offered only, 'I hope you have it insured. It really is worth a lot.'

'Insured? Yes. . . .' Trisha stopped staring wide-eyed at Raoul as the glimmering of an idea formed in her mind. He was looking back at her, his expression intense, but Trisha did not notice.

Salina had taken the record from the stereo and put on another. 'Darling, this is one of our songs,' she said, putting her hand through Raoul's arm and drawing him away from Trisha. 'Let's dance.'

Trisha watched them move away, a couple with everything going for them—good looks, wealth, a background of shared interests and common acquaintances. When Salina married Raoul she would face no major adjustments. Her life would continue in very much the same mould to which she was accustomed.

It seemed that pain at the thought of Raoul's marriage to another woman was inevitable. But this thought was not the only one in Trisha's mind. Moments ago there had been the germ of an idea, and now the idea was growing. As Trisha watched Raoul and Salina—the dark head and the fair one close together—she found herself trembling.

CHAPTER SEVEN

By next morning Trisha had decided to put the idea into effect. All that remained was to talk to Raoul, to tell him that she was leaving Vareen House. Nothing he could say would persuade her to stay. He had lost his hold over her—as Carl had done.

What would Carl say when he learned that she would not be doing the story? He would be furious, of course. Would he also understand, if only dimly, that she found it impossible to write about a girl as vulnerable as Paulie? That it was against all her principles to take advantage of the situation into which she had manoeuvred herself? Yet perhaps, after all, he would not understand, particularly if he knew that Raoul had agreed to the story in return for Trisha's help.

But Carl's anger was no longer the awesome factor it had once been. If her refusal made him decide that he no longer wanted to keep her at the paper, she would find herself another job. The main thing was that last night's idea had given her a new perspective, not only as it applied to Jerry's problems but also for the bearing it would have on her own life. With a certain measure of independence, there was no limit to the opportunities that all at once appeared possible.

Restlessly she stood at the open window and

stared out over the lovely garden. The sun was
shining on the hibiscus just beneath her, gilding
the scarlet petals so that they shone like burnished red gold, and a little way distant two brightly
plumaged parakeets were enjoying a noisy quarrel
in a palm tree. It was the beginning of another
shimmering tropical day, and she would not be at
Vareen House to enjoy it.

She would not leave, of course, without saying
her goodbyes. Goodbye to Gary, who had never
expected her to stay more than a few days. To
Paulie, who in such a short time had become a
friend. If only the friendship could continue, how
easy it would be to phone Paulie and suggest
further meetings. But Trisha knew that when she
had left Vareen House she would sever all ties
with the people who lived here.

Goodbye to Raoul—the most difficult farewell
of the lot. Would Raoul release her from her
promise? It would make the parting more difficult
if he did not, but his refusal would not alter her
decision. Short of putting her under lock and key,
there was little Raoul could do to keep her here.

Goodbye, Raoul. . . . Experimentally she tried
the words on her tongue, and found her lips were
dry. It was going to be very hard to say goodbye
to Raoul. The sooner she got it over the better.

But when she came down to breakfast Raoul
was nowhere to be seen. A casual enquiry elicited
the information that he had gone into Durban for
the day, that he was meeting Salina for dinner in
town that evening, and would not be back till very
late. Trisha's case was packed and she had

intended leaving soon after the meal; it was not easy for her to maintain a smiling composure.

For a moment she was tempted to go ahead with her plan. How simple it would be to leave Vareen House in Raoul's absence. Neither Gary nor Paulie would stop her. When Raoul returned he would be furious, but there would be nothing he could do.

It was a temptation she resisted. Reproaching herself for being a fool, she nevertheless felt that she owed it to Raoul to speak to him. Until she had done so she would say nothing to the others.

The day seemed unending, a bitter-sweet day. On one hand, having made up her mind to go, she was in a hurry to get done with it. On the other, she found herself savouring the sheer loveliness of the house and garden, the pleasure of being in the company of two such very nice people.

Evening came, and after Paulie had gone to bed Gary asked Trisha to walk with him in the garden. 'I've had so little time alone with you,' he said when she hesitated. Trisha went, and did not know which was more difficult, warding off Gary's attempts at lovemaking or the effort to push Raoul from her thoughts.

She was still thinking of Raoul long after she had said goodnight to Gary at the door of her room—a very firm goodnight, to indicate that she did not want him to come in. It was late, almost midnight, and she knew that Raoul had not yet returned.

Stop thinking about him, she told herself angrily. It doesn't matter that he's with Salina, that they're dining together, perhaps dancing. It doesn't matter that they'll drive home together along the quiet scented roads, that Salina will sit close to him and that he will have his arm around her shoulder. That later, when they get to Hazeldene, he'll kiss her with all the passion I have experienced. None of it matters, none of it! After tomorrow I'll never need to see Raoul Vareen again.

So she told herself. And still the thoughts kept coming, visions and images whirling in her mind until she thought she would go mad. With a little cry of unhappiness she clasped her hands to her eyes as if by so doing she could erase the pictures that tormented her.

The scream came suddenly—one scream, seconds later another. Trisha tore her hands from her eyes and sat up quickly. Paulie! The screams had surely come from Paulie. Footsteps sounded along the passage, and then a door creaked.

In seconds she was out of her bed and in Paulie's room. It was empty. Stopping only to run back to her room for slippers, Trisha ran down the stairs.

The front door was closed, the lock bolted. She made her way quickly to a side door, and found it ajar.

She stopped on the patch of grass beyond the door and stared into the darkness. The garden, always big, was a vast and mysterious place at night. The sky was overcast, with just the dim

light of the moon breaking through the clouds
to cast an eerie sheen over shifting shapes and
shadows.

Blinking eyes that were not yet attuned to the
dark, Trisha knew a few moments of despair.
Paulie was out here somewhere. But where? Her
screams had been terror-filled. Once before
Trisha had heard her scream, and then Paulie had
been having a nightmare. Raoul had comforted
her—somehow he had known how to deal with
the frightened girl. But Raoul was not here now.

Should she run inside and wake Gary? He too
might know what to do. But no, she rejected the
idea almost immediately. Waking Gary would
mean the loss of precious minutes in which Paulie
could come to harm. She must find the girl herself.

As her eyes grew accustomed to the darkness
she was able to make out more of her surroundings. Tentatively she took a few steps forward,
her eyes searching the shrub-filled vastness.
Paulie was out here somewhere; heaven only knew
where she was going.

A flicker of movement caught her eyes, a slight
white form moving rapidly on the east lawn.
Paulie . . . it had to be her. Startled, Trisha
realised that the girl was moving more rapidly
than she would have imagined possible. She
watched her a second, then she began to run.

Once she fell over a sprawling root, and for a
full minute she lay winded, shivering in her thin
nightgown on grass that was already moistened
with dew. Then she was up again. Paulie was no

longer in sight, but Trisha took the direction where she had last seen her. And all the while she called her name, 'Paulie! Paulie!'

In a clearing she saw her again, a slender wraith running over the grass, her hands extended at her sides. 'Paulie!' Trisha shouted. 'Paulie, stop!' but the girl did not respond, and it came to Trisha quite suddenly that Paulie was sleepwalking.

At last she caught up with her. Paulie tried to jerk away as Trisha took her arm, but Trisha held firm. The younger girl's face was terror-filled, her hair wild.

'Paulie. . . . Paulie, come back!'

'The wolf! Let me go! The wolf. . . .' The words emerged in an incoherent sob.

The same dream again—the wolf that had frightened her during her ordeal. Raoul had said Paulie had the same nightmare often.

'There's no wolf,' Trisha said as soothingly as she could. 'Paulie, you're dreaming. You're at home, at Vareen House. . . .'

'No! The wolf! Have to go. . . .'

How did one get a person to break free from a nightmare? Trisha thought of Raoul, and wished once more that he was here. Raoul was too sure of himself, but he would know what to do. He would know how to cope in almost any crisis, she thought fleetingly.

'Paulie, wake up. Paulie, I'm Trisha, your friend. Paulie, you're at home. . . .'

Gradually, very gradually, the girl did wake up. It was as if she came out of a trance. Blinking, she stared at Trisha, then around her at the dark garden.

'I.... How did I get here?' she whispered.

'You had a dream.'

'The wolf....'

'The wolf,' Trisha agreed gently. 'Paulie, let's get back.'

Paulie began to shiver, a shivering that began slowly, then increased as it spread to all her body. Sobs came from her throat. 'Always the wolf,' she gasped.

'I know.' Trisha felt a great welling of compassion as she put her arm around Paulie's shoulders. 'You're cold.'

'So cold....'

'Come, Paulie, let's get back to the house.'

They had gone a little way when Trisha noticed that Paulie was limping, and looking down she saw that the girl's feet were bare.

'Don't you have shoes?' she asked, and realised the futility of her question in the same instant. Paulie had been sleepwalking, she would not have thought to wear shoes.

'You're limping,' she said.

A helpless gesture. 'Yes.'

'I wonder if there's another way....' Trisha gave a sudden gasp as she remembered the wounds left on Paulie's feet by the cigarettes. 'Your feet! Here...' she bent and hastily took off her slippers, 'wear these.'

'I can't.' Paulie hung back in protest. 'They're yours.'

'Please, you must.' And as the younger girl

reluctantly pulled on the slippers, 'That's right. You're shivering, Paulie. My golly, the sooner you get back into bed the better!'

They came to a path that was ornamental gravel, the stones were sharp and uneven beneath Trisha's feet. Stifling a cry of pain as a stone cut into her, she glanced around. There had to be a better way of negotiating this last stretch to the house. Bordering the path the trees were thick and dark, and Trisha looked at them doubtfully, wondering if it would be possible to go through them. She had half turned towards them when a low cry rang through the night, the hunting call of a night-bird. She shuddered, and propelled Paulie forward along the stony path.

They were almost at the house when a figure materialised in the darkness, and Trisha stood still with shock. And then he spoke, 'Paulie? Trisha?' and she relaxed in sudden relief. She had never been more glad to see him.

'Raoul!'

'You're all right?' He was beside them now and was bending towards Paulie.

'Raoul, it was horrible ... the wolf again. ...' The sob was back in Paulie's voice. 'I tried to get away. ...'

'You walked in your sleep?'

'Yes. Oh, Raoul!'

'And Trisha came after you.' Not a question, just a quiet statement. Raoul knew what had happened, just as he would always know anything of importance pertaining to the people who meant something to him.

'Yes. She gave me her slippers.' Paulie gestured to her feet. 'Raoul, it was so awful!'

'I know, dear.' He turned slightly. 'And you, Trisha, are you all right?'

'Yes.' The unaccustomed warmth she saw in his face filled her with fleeting happiness. 'How did you know where we were?'

'It wasn't difficult. The house was in darkness, but the bedroom doors were open, so I went into Paulie's room. . . .'

'You looked into mine too?' The words were out before she could stop them, and she was glad it was too dark for him to see the flush that suddenly stained her cheeks.

He nodded. For a moment his gaze held hers in the darkness, then he was turning to Paulie once more. 'Come, dear, I want you to get inside.'

At the door of Paulie's room they parted company. The younger girl hugged her impulsively. 'Thank you, Trisha.'

'Can I do anything more to help?'

'No,' Raoul answered for his sister. 'You look almost as cold as this child here. I'll see to her. Get to bed, Trisha.' He paused, then said, 'And thank you.'

Her feet were even more cut up than she'd realised, Trisha saw when she put on the light. She should bathe them, but she was suddenly very tired; cold too. The tropical nights were normally only a little less hot than the days, but tonight had been different, the air had been cool and a breeze had chilled her scantily-clad body.

Wearily she sat down on the bed. In a while

she would clean the grazes. It was silly to delay, for she was leaving tomorrow, and she wanted to make an early start after talking to all three Vareens. It was so late, and she should get to bed. But still she sat.

At the sound of knocking, she turned her head. Rigidly she stared at the door. The knocking came again, then Raoul called softly, 'Please open the door, Trisha.'

'What are you doing here?' she asked when he had come inside.

He closed the door quietly behind him. 'You knew I'd come.'

She had known it. Deep inside her she *had* known it. She looked at him, taking in every detail of the face that she would not see again after to-morrow, and she was unable to speak.

'You did know I'd come,' he insisted, still quietly. 'I want to thank you, Trisha.'

She swallowed over the lump in her throat. 'You did already. And . . . it was no more than anyone would have done.'

'I don't know about that.' He had never looked at her in quite this way. It was a look that sent her heart racing. 'I think you did a pretty wonderful thing,' he said.

It was hard to meet his gaze. 'Paulie had to be helped.'

'You could have called Gary.' His voice changed. 'And there was no reason to give Paulie your slippers.'

'Her feet. . . .'

'You were thinking of her wounds,' he said

quietly. 'You put Paulie's feet before your own.'

'It was the natural thing to do,' she said
shakily.

'For a hardboiled newspaper-woman only out
for a story?' He took hold of her hands, drawing
her a little closer to him.

'Y-Yes.'

'I think,' he said very softly, and so close to her
that she felt the warmth of his breath fan her hair,
'that your actions were those of a girl who cares
about people. About Paulie.'

'I do care about Paulie.'

'I know, and I'm grateful.' Giving her no time
to reflect on such an extraordinary statement from
Raoul Vareen, he went on, 'Let me see your feet.'

'My feet?' She drew back as far as his hands
allowed her. 'No, Raoul.'

'Yes,' he insisted. 'Sit down on the bed.'

The heartbeat that had slowed moments earlier
was now racing wildly. 'Why?'

'To satisfy my curiosity.'

Still she hung back. She *could not* lift her feet
for Raoul's inspection. And then she gasped,
caught unprepared as Raoul lifted her from the
ground. For what seemed an interminable
moment he held her against him, so close that she
could feel the hard tautness of him, then he put
her on the bed and sat down next to her.

'Are you always so stubborn?' His laugh was
husky.

'Wh-when necessary.'

'And how does dull George deal with your
stubbornness?' A hand went to her face, brushing

a cheek, sliding softly around one ear before moving to her forehead where it pushed back a fallen strand of hair. 'Don't tell me,' he said, 'I can guess. He would never force you to do anything.'

'Don't knock him,' Trisha said through numb lips.

'I'm not knocking him. I've no doubt George is a gentleman. He gives in to your whims and never argues with your opinions.'

'What's wrong with that?' she demanded.

'He's solid and respectable and the soul of honour.'

'Unlike you, Raoul.'

'His kisses are chaste, and he never strikes a chord of abandon in your very warm-blooded feminine body.'

He was so close to the truth that Trisha could not answer. Malice aside, Raoul had described George sight unseen. She knew she should be outraged, that she should counter his audaciousness with a stinging retort, and to her horror she found that she had to compress her lips tightly to prevent herself from laughing.

The laughter died in her as Raoul turned his attention to her feet. There was no avoiding him as he lifted first one foot, then the other, turning them downside up and cradling them in his hands. She heard his intake of breath, and saw his throat work.

'Worse than I thought,' he said, his eyes returning to her face.

'I . . . was just about to wash them.'

'I'll do that.'

She made a small helpless gesture. 'No, Raoul.'

'Yes, stubborn one.' And as she tried to move away from him, 'Don't you understand? I want to do it.'

'Why, Raoul, why?' she demanded, as he began to wipe away the gravel.

'Don't you know, Trisha?'

His movements were gentle. A nurse could not have been more careful. A few gashes were deeper than she'd imagined, but as Raoul cleaned them he did not hurt her.

'Trisha?'

The way in which he said her name set her pulses racing. What could be more mundane than having a few grazes cleaned and bandaged, yet these moments with Raoul were filled with an unnerving sensuousness—a sensuousness which she did not understand. A little wildly Trisha wondered if what she felt was imaginary, or if Raoul felt it too.

She forced a light tone. 'Because of Paulie?' she suggested.

The smooth dark head was bent over her feet, but at her words it lifted. The eyes that looked into hers were narrowed and enigmatic, hard to read. Trisha held her breath as she waited for Raoul to speak, but he did not. For a moment that seemed endless he looked at her, his eyes defying hers to shift away, then his lips curved just a little, as if something in her face gave him cause for amusement—or satisfaction. When Trisha thought she could hold her breath no longer he bent his head once more, directing his attention back to her feet.

At length he said, 'Are you really the hard-boiled newspaper-woman you pretend to be?'

The question, as much as the huskiness of his tone, took her by surprise. Trisha's heart did a double beat, then slowed again. 'What else?'

Again the dark head lifted. This time the eyes beneath the thick winging brows gleamed. 'That, my dear Trisha, is something I will take pleasure in finding out.'

She stared at him. 'Now?'

'No, stubborn one. In the next few days.'

'I don't understand. . . .' she began.

'We're going on a trip.'

'No!'

'Into the interior,' he said, as if he had not heard her.

'I am not. . . .'

'To the place where Paulie was hidden.' He paused, and this time she did not interrupt him. His lips curved once more, in a genuine smile this time. 'I'm glad I caught your interest.'

Oh yes, she was interested all right. Not that it made any difference. She would be gone from here long before the intended trip was to take place.

'Tonight decided me,' Raoul continued. 'There've been too many nightmares—now the sleepwalking. It's time to take a look at the place where Paulie was kept.'

'You can't believe in the wolf.'

'No. We both know there are no wolves in

Africa, but that's not the point. Paulie believes in it.'

'Yes. . . .'

'There must be something. It's so vivid in her mind—an animal at the mouth of the cave, howling and barking.'

'You don't think she imagined it?' Trisha asked thoughtfully.

'I think she believed what she was told. Something was there all right, and we're going to find out what it was.'

Trisha looked away, unwilling now to meet his eyes. Very slowly, she managed, 'I won't be going with you.'

'I want you there.'

So easily said, with so much confidence. Did it ever occur to Raoul that people would not always fall in with his wishes? Did Salina do everything that he asked?

'I won't be here, Raoul.'

There, she had said it. She tensed, waiting for him to reply. After a few seconds of silence she looked up. He was watching her, his expression taut, his eyes intense.

'Didn't you hear what I said? I won't be here—I'm leaving in the morning. I'd have left yesterday, but I waited for you to come back. I want you to release me from my promise.'

'Why?' His tone was without expression. And when she remained silent, unable to answer, 'Anything to do with me?'

Yes, yes, yes! Everything to do with you. I can't bear to go on staying here in the same house with you. Aware of you every waking moment. Tortured by my imagination. Loving you. . . .

Loving you! Yes, I love you. I don't know when I began to love you, but I do, and I hate it. You're not the kind of man I'd have chosen to love. I can't imagine sharing a life with you, and I can't bear to contemplate life without you. And whatever I imagine is futile anyway, because there can never be a future with you.

'Trisha, answer me.'

'Nothing to do with you,' she answered, her voice low and controlled.

'You don't have your story. Not yet.'

'Perhaps it's not necessary any more.'

'There's something you're not telling me.' He had finished with her feet. His hands were moving over her now, slowly, tantalisingly, exploring the shape of her, curving around her hips, her waist, her arms, sending flames along her nerve-stream, making her throb with the stirring of desire.

Somehow she suppressed the longing to bury her hands in the dark hair. Her nerves had never felt more fragile. She managed to lie very still while the long fingers moved over her skin, leaving behind a trail that burned and tingled.

'Tell me, Trisha,' Raoul said softly.

'Isn't it enough that I want to leave?' she whispered.

'We've gone too far for that. I want you to come on this trip, Trisha.'

'No! I can't.' She was unable to conceal her trembling as Raoul bent and let his lips brush against the swell of breast above the line of her nightgown.

'Gary. . . .' She was improvising desperately now. 'Gary might come in. . . . And on the trip. . . . He's jealous.'

'We'll have to contend with that.'

'But you said. . . .'

'I know what I said,' Raoul said softly. 'Gary fancies himself in love with you. He sees our closeness and is jealous. I don't like it, Trisha, but it's happened.'

'I have to get away from it,' she insisted.

'Not now.'

'But Gary. . . .'

'. . . . will get over his infatuation,' he finished for her. 'My brother falls in love easily. He gets over a broken heart just as quickly. There's always another eager girl around.'

Do you get over a broken heart with equal ease? And have you ever been in love? Truly in love? Do you love Salina?

'Gary. . . .' She stopped, and looked at Raoul, unaware that her eyes were very big, luminous in the glow of the bedside light, and that her lips trembled. Unaware that to the man who sat beside her on the bed she looked almost as vulnerable as the sister who had walked in terror just half an hour earlier.

'Raoul, I want to leave here,' she said. 'I don't know what else to say.'

'But there's something *I* want to say.'

She looked at him, and felt a quiver tremble through her.

'*I* want you to stay, Trisha. *I* want you—for myself; for both of us.'

'You don't know what you're saying.' The words emerged painfully.

Long fingers moved over her upper arms, stroking, caressing, adding fire to existing flames. 'Yes, Trisha, I do know. There is something between us.' Numbly she shook her head. 'Yes, my stubborn one, you know it as well as I do. Admit it, Trisha.'

She wanted to say yes. God, how she wanted to say yes! But if she did she would also tell him that she loved him, and that would be inviting his ridicule, and ridicule was the one thing she could not accept—not from Raoul.

'Trisha, admit it. We *are* attracted to each other.'

Little point in denying it. Her body had spoken for her so often in the past. He had only to touch her, to feel the hardening response of her body, to know what she felt. As for Raoul—he was attracted to her, she knew that too. But the attraction was a physical thing, the need of a man for a woman. Raoul did not love her as she loved him. If he loved any woman, she was Salina. In the circumstances Trisha would admit nothing.

'Trisha!'

'Anything I could say would be meaningless,' she got out through a tight throat.

'Is that what you think? Is it? See if this is meaningless.'

His head swooped low, and before she could stop him his lips were crushing down on hers. The kiss was hungry, it was sensual and exploring as his mouth opened hers, and any thought of resistance vanished as desire stirred within her once more, a desire that was not unlike a raw and aching pain. She loved this man, no matter what his feelings were for her—and more and more she craved the fulfilment of physical expression.

There was glory in the meeting of mouths, in the closeness of his body against hers. His arms encircled her back and he was bending over her, his chest a burning imprint against her breasts. His mouth left hers to explore her face, shaping her cheeks, her nose, the corners of her eyes, and all the while her own lips made a rapturous exploration of their own—it was one thing to have his features branded like fire on her mind, another to learn the feel of them.

He lifted her nightgown away from her so that he could cup first one breast and then the other in his fingers, caressing the responding firmness. Such was the erotic pleasure he gave her that Trisha let out an involuntary moan, and then she was caressing him too, pushing her hands beneath the silk shirt, sliding them over the hard muscles of his back and shoulders, the flatness of his stomach, and the blood sang in her veins.

When Raoul lifted himself away from her it was as if something very precious had been taken from her. He looked down at her, his breathing still slightly ragged. 'There is something between us, Trisha. You have to admit it.'

I love you, she thought. But if I tell you that I will see contempt in your eyes and hear the words of disbelief on your lips, and I couldn't bear that.

'Chemistry,' she said on a laugh that was more like a sob.

His expression changed, and the long firm jaw seemed to clench. For just a moment the hand on her breast tightened, then relaxed. 'We can call it chemistry if you want,' he agreed, his voice a little rough. 'Whatever, it exists. I can't let you go away, Trisha.'

If only you meant it as I do. I don't want to go, don't you know that? I want to stay here always, share your life, be a part of your joys and sorrows, be part of *you*. But for all of that you have Salina.

'I feel I must go,' she insisted in a small voice.

'Just a few days.' His tone had changed again, its coolness disturbing. 'I want to make the trip to the cave, and I want you to be there. A woman's presence—it could be important.'

I will not go, you can't expect it of me. But the words that emerged, almost without volition, were, 'If you need me I'll be there.'

CHAPTER EIGHT

THEY left at dawn two days later. Raoul drove the station-wagon, Paulie was beside him. Trisha and Gary were in the back seat.

Almost immediately Gary reached for Trisha's hand. Her instinct was to withdraw it for the sensation of Gary's hand on hers gave her no joy—and that was strange, for she still thought of Gary as one of the nicest men she had met. But perhaps it was not strange at all, perhaps hereafter physical contact with any man but Raoul would be distasteful. If that were so, she thought unhappily, the future was indeed bleak. The departure from Vareen House had merely been postponed. When this trip ended she could delay it no longer. With her return to Durban Raoul would vanish from her life. If the mere thought of contact with another man made her ill the years ahead would be lonely.

As if he sensed her reaction, Gary's grip tightened. Looking at him, Trisha saw that the line of his jaw was grim. In the half-light he looked not unlike his brother. If she withdrew from him now he might well create a scene; so she left her hand in his and turned to the window.

They had left the estate and were driving through farmlands. In the daylight the steel blue of the sky and the tropical nature of the vegetation

created a land of stunning colour. Now, in the
dim light of early morning, the landscape was very
different. Trees laden with mangoes and pawpaws, with peaches and plums and nectarines,
were ghostly shapes in the greyness, and Natal's
rolling hills were humped silhouettes against the
slowly lightening sky. Over the land lay an air of
brooding mystery that blended with Trisha's
mood.

Without meaning to she glanced at the figure
in the seat in front of her. She saw the confident
thrust of the throat, the width of the shoulders,
the thickness of the dark hair that just touched
the top of a mohair sweater. Even now, when she
could see so little of him, she was struck by
Raoul's maleness, his virility, and a familiar sensation quivered inside her.

In the driving mirror she saw Raoul's eyes. He
was looking at her, she realised quite suddenly,
just as she was looking at him, and the shock of
the realisation must have registered on her face,
for she saw his eyes crinkle in amusement. At the
same moment the grip on her hand became even
tighter, and tension was communicated from
Gary's arm to her own. So Gary had not missed
the silent interchange.

Confused, Trisha turned her face back to the
window. There was tension in this car, not just
Gary's tension, but a quality that was alive and
tingling and so real that she felt as if she could
touch it. Let this trip end quickly, she prayed.
Let it live up to Raoul's expectations so that
Paulie comes away from it healed, and then let us

all go our separate ways. The sooner we get back into the streams of our own lives once more the better.

The sun rose and the air grew hot. Raoul turned on the air-conditioning and the radio, and Trisha was glad. The lively music of a new country and western group made small-talk unnecessary.

Outside the window the landscape was changing. For a while the car had followed a coastal road, now it was travelling inland. Sugar country this was, a constant vista of undulating land, rolling hills and gentle valleys, every inch of it covered in sugar cane, mile upon mile of sugar cane. The long bamboo-like shoots stood close together, the feather-like foliage spreading above them in an endless sea of green and gold. Now and then a breeze swept the land, and then the cane bent and straightened in waves that rippled to the horizon and beyond.

How lovely Natal was, Trisha thought, and how much more she would enjoy this drive if not for the atmosphere in the car.

Paulie had spoken very little, and Trisha wondered what was in the girl's mind as she set out to revisit the scene of her ordeal, but she thought it best not to ask. Sitting beside Raoul, Paulie looked even smaller and paler than usual. She had the air of one who had withdrawn to a place where none could follow.

As the scenery changed yet again, the cane fields giving way to a landscape that was bleak and windswept and completely uncultivated, Paulie stirred. There was a jerkiness in her movements as she turned her head from one side to the other. 'We're there?' she asked in a voice that was shrill with emotion.

'Almost, dear,' Raoul answered in the gentle tone that surprised Trisha each time she heard it.

'Let's go back!'

'No, dear.'

'Please! Raoul, I'm frightened.'

'I want you to see the cave, Paulie.'

'But . . . .' Paulie stopped. She covered her eyes and began to cry.

Withdrawing her hand from Gary's, Trisha leaned forward and stroked the soft brown hair. 'Paulie, we're all with you—Raoul and Gary and I.' And as the girl continued to weep, 'We'll be with you all the time. We won't let you be hurt.'

Paulie did not answer. Trisha continued to stroke her hair and gradually the weeping lessened. At length Trisha sat back in her seat. Without thinking her eyes went to the rear-view mirror. Raoul was watching her—waiting for her! As their eyes met he smiled, and she saw that his expression was warm with approval. Happiness surged through her, and she smiled back.

They drove farther and she looked with growing interest at a landscape that was so devoid of any life, human or animal, that kidnappers had been able to keep a girl hidden, secure in the knowledge that she would not be found.

'I remember it all,' Paulie said presently, her voice ragged from her weeping. She turned to look at Trisha. 'It was so awful—so frightening! The way they grabbed me just when I was getting out of the car—they must have known Raoul and. Gary were not at home that day, and as it was a Sunday all the servants were out.'

Don't relive it, Trisha wanted to say, her heart going out to the girl with the matted eyelashes and the wan distraught face. But she remained silent. It was good that Paulie could talk, that she could verbalise what had tormented her for so long.

'They blindfolded me and then they threw me into the back of the car. I pleaded with them . . . cried, but they wouldn't listen. Later, it seemed like hours later, they took off the blindfold. Perhaps they felt sorry for me. Whatever, I remember this place.' She fell silent again, and now her face was turned to the window.

At a pile of rock Raoul switched off the ignition. 'This is as far as the road goes,' he announced. 'Remember this too, Paulie?'

'Yes . . . yes, I think so.'

'May as well get out,' said Gary.

Trisha was relieved to be leaving the confines of the station-wagon, glad to be able to stretch her legs. A breeze stirred the hot air, cooling her skin.

Only Paulie was reluctant to leave the vehicle. 'I . . . don't think I want to,' she whispered as Raoul looked at her questioningly.

Trisha registered the unspoken fear. 'You're thinking of the wolf?' She glanced at Raoul, then back at Paulie. 'There are no wolves in Africa, dear.' Unconsciously she used Raoul's endearment for his sister.

'Maybe a jackal,' said Gary. 'There *are* jackals

around here. Or a hyena, perhaps?'

Paulie shuddered and Trisha took her hand. Gently but firmly she drew her out of the station-wagon as Raoul said, 'Let's not speculate. Let's get down to the cave.'

The scrub was thorny and hard underfoot as they began to walk. Twenty minutes brought them to the edge of a gorge. Trisha gasped as she looked down and took a step backwards; she had not realised that she stood by a precipice. The land dropped away in a long sheer line to rise again fifty feet farther. At the foot of the gorge, far, far below, a river was a thin snaking thread. Trees clung to the sides of the precipice, thin trees that straggled up towards the light, their roots sprawling above the rocky surface.

'It's incredible!' Trisha exclaimed.

'It's breathtaking,' Raoul agreed quietly from a point close beside her. 'You're very close to the edge.' His hand closed over her arm. It was a cautionary movement, she knew that, and yet she was powerless to prevent the weakness that took her.

'All right?' Perceptive eyes searched her face.

No, she wanted to say. There must be some-thing very wrong if I feel overcome each time you're near me. 'Just a bit dizzy from the height, I expect,' she said aloud.

'The cave's a little farther on. Gary and Paulie have gone on ahead.'

'Let's catch up with them, then.' Her voice was as matter-of-fact as she could make it.

'Notebook and pencil all ready?'

So he still believed she was only out for a story. Her chin lifted at the provocation in his tone. 'I keep my notes in my head.'

'Keen to do the most for your paper?'

'Avid.' No point in telling him that the story would never be written. 'Every gory detail.'

'Strange,' he said reflectively, 'that you wanted to leave us. Was that just a tactic of some sort?'

'Maybe.' The conversation hurt, but she had to go on with it. 'But I'm here now and I'll get lots of material.'

'Then you are hardboiled after all.' There was an odd inflection in his tone. 'Just when I thought perhaps. . . .'

'Perhaps what?' she asked, suddenly breathless.

'Nothing.' His voice was abrupt. 'Come on, Trisha, let's walk.'

The cave was a little way farther. It was a hole in the side of a cliff almost covered with scrub. No wonder the kidnappers had felt safe, Trisha thought. The cave would be virtually invisible to a casual passer-by—if anybody ever came near this desolate spot. She wondered how Raoul had managed to find it. She turned to ask him, but one look at a face that was stern and closed kept her silent.

After some coaxing Paulie entered the cave. It was small and dark and uncomfortable, an awful place for a girl to be hidden for more than two weeks. Trisha felt a burning anger at the thought that one human could subject another to such a senseless ordeal. But there was no sign of an animal, either in the cave or around it.

They did not stay there long. Trisha saw that just a few minutes were a terrible strain for Paulie. She had been trembling when she entered the darkness, and when they came out she was even paler than before.

Raoul cast a tight-lipped look at his sister, then remarked, 'I think we'll go back to the station-wagon now and find a place to set up camp.

'Can't we go home?' Paulie's face was filled with pleading.

'Not today, dear. You might want to see the cave once more . . . tomorrow.'

'No! I never want to see it again!'

'We'll stay just in case.'

Paulie looked very close to tears and Gary was frowning, about to take his sister's part, Trisha thought. Quickly she said, 'Raoul's right, Paulie. You might feel better tomorrow, more relaxed and rested. And you really may want just one last look.'

'Well, just one more day, then.' Paulie gave in reluctantly.

They walked back in silence to the spot where the station-wagon had been parked. Paulie still looked wrought-up, Gary disappointed. Raoul's expression was different. The handsome face was set in hard spare lines, and the grey eyes were as thoughtful as Trisha had seen them. She wondered what he was thinking.

They climbed into the vehicle and then Raoul drove back some way to a spot where they could put up the tents. 'Will we have a campfire?' Paulie asked, brightening just a little.

'Sure,' said Gary. 'Might as well enjoy ourselves while we're here. A braai, a few songs before we turn in.' His voice seemed purposely bright, as if in some way he was trying to compensate his sister for the disappointment of finding nothing.

What had they thought they would see in the cave? Trisha wondered.

The two men worked quickly. In no time the tents had been pegged, and the camping gear was set out. Lifting the lid of the cool-box Trisha saw steak packed on ice, and boerewors and a bottle of wine. Whoever planned the expedition had thought of everything.

'Let's find wood,' she heard Raoul say, and they spread out to all sides.

Trisha made in the direction of the gorge. She went slowly, gathering dry wood as she went. Near the edge of the gorge she stopped. Awed by the height of the precipice, she was nevertheless fascinated by the sheer magnificence of the sight. Dared she go any closer? Yes, just one step. . . .

'Careful,' said a voice at her shoulder, and a hand gripped her arm as she jerked round.

'Raoul!' she exclaimed shakily. 'That's the second time you've pulled me back.' And then, on a firmer note, 'You frightened me.'

'Better that than that you should have fallen over the edge.' At the roughness in his tone a tremor shot through her.

'I was just looking,' she said. She had taken another step away from the edge now, but his

hand was still on her arm. 'It's the strangest place
I ever saw, Raoul.'

'As if a giant sickle had been dragged along the
bowels of the earth.'

'You've just put into words the thought that
was in my mind.' She stared up at him, eyes shining. 'It's not the first time you've done that.'

A hand cupped her chin, the fingers burning
where they touched her throat. 'It's not?' he asked
softly.

'You seem to ... to understand. . . .' She
stopped, confused.

'Perhaps I do.' The pressure of his fingers increased just a fraction. 'I'd like to think that I do.'

She turned away, feeling strangely unsettled.
'It's so beautiful,' she murmured with a vague
gesture.

'Very beautiful.' His hand was still beneath her
chin, and now he moved her head around so that
she faced him once more. There was a slight curve
to lips that she was coming to know almost better
than her own, and his eyes glittered. He was so
close to her that she could see the warm flecks in
the blue of his eyes. 'Very beautiful,' he said
again, softly, in a tone that indicated he was talking about something other than the gorge. Could
he feel the sudden racing of her pulses beneath
his thumb? Trisha wondered.

This was a different Raoul from the one she
had thought she knew—much nicer, yet still ex-
citing and dangerous. I love you, she thought,
sending the silent message across the inches that
separated them, but I don't know how to cope

with my feelings. I don't know how to cope with *you*.

'Paulie seems reassured,' she said, driven by the need to change to a safe topic.

'Do you really think so?' The hand had dropped from her chin, and Trisha did not know if she was glad.

'Well, yes. The cave was so ordinary. Bleak and small and darned uncomfortable—but ordinary.'

'Too ordinary.' Raoul had turned away and was staring into the gorge, a tall lithe figure, masculine and devastatingly attractive even now, when his profile was stern.

'You're thinking of the wolf. . . .'

'Of course.' He swung back, and she saw that the warmth had left his eyes. 'If all we saw was an empty cave we achieved nothing.'

'There can't be a wolf.'

'But there is something—or was. Paulie has never been neurotic.'

She looked at him. The setting sun was behind him, its rays had caught his head and made of it a sculpted thing of burnished bronze. 'You know the answer,' she said on a sudden wave of feminine instinct.

He hesitated. 'I have a theory.'

'Tell me.'

'When I've tested it.' He bent to pick up a stone. He tossed it over the side of the precipice, and was silent as the stone clattered along the bumpy rock-face. When the last echo had died away he said, 'I mean to put it to the test tonight.'

She stared at him. 'We're going to the cave?'

'*I*'m going.'

Fear caught in her throat. 'Alone?'

'Yes.'

'No!' she protested.

'Yes. Don't say a word to the others.'

Without thinking she put a hand on his arm, and felt the muscle beneath it grow tight. 'Let me come with you.'

'No, Trisha.' He put out a finger and traced a soft line along her nose and around each of her eyes. She had to force herself to stand very still as her body was swept with a stab of longing. Gary could so easily appear through the bush, looking for her. Now was not the moment to give in to the craving to wrap her arms around Raoul's waist and press herself against him.

'I'm going alone,' he said.

They were walking back to the campsite, dry wood in their arms, when he spoke again. 'We all owe you thanks.' And when she stopped to look at him, 'You've been good with Paulie.'

'I've done very little,' she shrugged.

'You've done more than you realise. Paulie's been so much more relaxed since you've been with us. Today you smoothed some very difficult moments.'

Trisha stopped walking and lifted her face to him, filled with the happiness his approval brought every time. Green eyes were luminous as she said, 'I'm glad.'

He was watching her, his expression enigmatic, 'You've earned your story.'

The happiness drained from her as suddenly as if she had been a balloon that had been pricked by a pin. Amazing that she could have forgotten, even for a moment, the real nature of her relationship with the Vareens, in particular with the man who had become so important to her.

'Yes, well,' she said lightly, 'it will be a good story. Especially if your theory—whatever it is—proves correct.'

The sun dipped beneath the horizon in a blaze of colour that was as short as it was spectacular. In those minutes the nature of the countryside was transformed. Dour rock-face glowed in a sheen of rose and purple, and the shapes of leafless trees were blurred and softened.

In Africa it gets dark quickly once the sun has set. By the time the fire was lit darkness had fallen and the shrilling of the crickets was a constant sound upon the still air.

If Paulie had been affected by the visit to the cave, she did not show it as she helped Trisha prepare steak and boerewors for the flames. Not once did she refer to her ordeal, but chatted instead about other things. Gary too, after an initial compressing of lips when he saw Trisha and Raoul returning together to the campsite, was relaxed and talkative.

Trisha wondered if only she noticed that Raoul was silent and that he seemed unusually preoccupied. She was filled with a sense of uneasiness which she could not dispel. Somehow she forced herself to partake of the braaivleis, to respond to the chatter of Gary and Paulie, yet as the hours passed her tension grew. Now and then she caught Raoul's eyes in the flickering light of the fire. It was too dark to read their expression, but she thought she caught a look of warning, as if he said again, 'I'm going to the cave alone.'

Durban and its surroundings are usually hot night and day, but this desolate place was different. With almost no vegetation to retain the day's heat, it grew cold with the going of the sun. When the fire died the two girls were shivering. 'Time for bed,' said Raoul, and jerking round to look at him, Trisha caught the warning expression once more.

Paulie was soon asleep. In her sleeping-bag Trisha lay awake, her ears straining for the sound of footsteps. Raoul would wait until he was certain that all were asleep, then he would go.

The tension which had been with her all evening had grown worse. The cave had been a dismal enough place in the daytime; what would it be like at night? And what would Raoul find there? Not a wolf, she knew that—but what? What? And would he be in danger?

The idea came quite suddenly, the decision seconds later. For a long moment she lay quite still, the breath stilled in her lungs. Dared she do it? Could she? And what would Raoul say if she did? Would he be furious? Yes, he would, but it would not matter, for it would be too late for him to do anything about it. On an indrawn breath of elation she sat up.

It was very quiet as she crept out of the tent.

There was no movement from the tent just yards away. The moon was almost full, as Raoul had said it would be, and in its light Trisha saw the station-wagon. Thank God—she had not waited too long.

As silently as she could she made her way over the prickly scrub. She reached the station-wagon and found it unlocked. A sign from the fates that she had made the right decision? Still keeping her movements quiet, she opened the back door and lay flat on the floor of the vehicle.

She had been there more than ten minutes when the front door was opened and something landed on top of her. Raoul's jacket—she would have recognised it even if she had not known that it was Raoul who had got into the station-wagon— the jacket was a rough tweed, and the odour that clung to it was one that she had come to associate with Raoul, one that was earthily male. There was joy in the feel of the jacket on her face. In some way it was as if she was close to its owner. There was added warmth too, a welcome warmth in the coldness of the vehicle.

As the station-wagon lurched over the bumpy road, Trisha was glad that the drive would be short. Raoul stopped the car, then reached an arm backwards for his jacket. His hand stiffened as it made contact with the form beneath the garment, and then the jacket was jerked upwards and a face was peering down at Trisha from the front seat.

'It's you!' he exclaimed.

'Raoul. . . .' A tentative murmur.

'You silly little daredevil!' There was anger in

his tone, exasperation too.

'Don't be mad!' she protested.

'You ask so little,' he said mockingly. 'Sit up, Trisha, and stop looking so demure, you're anything but. Yes, that's better. Now tell me what I should do with you.'

'Take me with you.'

Unexpectedly he laughed, a low amused sound, seductive in the cool darkness. Then he had opened his door and hers and was reaching for her, jerking her out of the car. 'Impossible girl,' he growled.

'I know,' she said, mock-prim.

His arm went around her shoulders, pulling her close against the hard side of him. 'Dull George will never cope with you. He won't, you do know that?'

'*You* know it.' A little hammer of excitement pounded in her temples.

'You know it too, daredevil.' The way he said it, the word had the sound of an endearment. 'Gary wouldn't be able to cope with you either—I've told you that before.'

But you would, Raoul. You would cope with me.

'Why did you stow away?' And then, giving her no chance to answer, he said in a changed tone, 'To get your own way, of course. Do you always get what you want, Trisha?'

No, I don't. There's one thing I want above all else, and that's beyond my reach. Because you don't want me, Raoul, not in the way that I want you.

'Sometimes,' she murmured.

'Why did you come?'

What would he say if she told him? For one dangerous moment Trisha was tempted to try the truth, then she said, 'You know why—the story.'

'Ah, the story.' She was so close to him that she could feel his voice in his chest.

'All the details . . . first-hand.' Her own voice was bumpy.

He stopped walking and moved her in his arms, turning her to face him. 'Why *did* you come, Trisha?'

'You . . . you kn—know the reason.' She was stammering, nervous all at once.

'Do I?' He made an impatient sound in his throat as he pulled her even closer. His jacket was sensuously rough against her face, the smell of it threatening to overwhelm her. One hand went to her hair, drawing back her head. In the moonlight he looked dangerous and more handsome than she had seen him.

'I want the real reason,' he said softly.

The softness was her undoing. She did not want to hold back the truth, she knew that now, and no matter the consequences. 'You could be in danger,' she said simply.

Raoul stared down at her, and for a long moment he did not speak. His breath was warm against her cold cheek. Then he said, 'So that's why you came?'

'Yes.' She did not know why tears welled suddenly in her eyes, did not know either that he could see them in the moonlight.

'You thought I'd be in danger?'

'You don't know what you'll find. I didn't want you to go alone.'

'I'd like to believe that. God, how I'd like to believe that! Daredevil—adorable little daredevil.

'Believe it,' she whispered.

In a strange tone he said, 'Perhaps I do.'

And then he was kissing her—deep hungry kisses. One hand was still in her hair, the other was on her hips, moulding her to him. Her mouth had opened to his, willingly, eagerly, and she was returning his kisses with an abandon that was a product of a deep longing. Her arms were around him, her hands sliding to his neck, his shoulders, as she cherished the shape of him.

'No more,' Raoul muttered hoarsely as he put her a little away from him. 'You're so lovely, Trisha. But if we go on now I might not be able to stop.'

I don't want to stop! I want you, Raoul.

'And we have to stop,' he said as if her own need had communicated itself to him. 'If we don't we won't get to the cave.'

The cave. . . . She had forgotten about it. 'Yes,' she said brittly, 'we must get to the cave.'

As they had done earlier in the day, they walked from the station-wagon to the cave. In the dark the going seemed more hazardous, the way longer, but Trisha did not mind. Raoul's arm was around her, and her head was against his shoulder, very lightly, so lightly that she wondered if he felt it. Twice when she would have fallen his arm tightened. The scream of a bird shrilled suddenly through the night.

'Nervous?' asked Raoul.

She was not nervous at all. With Raoul's arm around her, holding her, guiding her, she felt safe. Any woman would be safe with him, she thought. Lucky Salina, who would know the security of being always with Raoul, able to lean on him whenever she had to.

But tonight there was no Salina. There were only the two of them, Trisha and Raoul, quite alone in this desolate place.

'I'm not nervous,' she said. She looked up at him smiling.

'I should have known.' The hand on her shoulder tightened. 'You're quite a girl, Trisha. Careful now, we're nearly there.'

The cave was very dark. Even in the moonlight it had an intense and brooding darkness. Standing inside it, close to the reassuring safety of Raoul, Trisha felt a sense of identity with the girl who had been kept here forcibly. How terrified she must have been! Again Trisha experienced a terrible anger at the men who had brought Paulie here.

'God, this is awful,' she breathed. 'No punishment could be severe enough.'

'I agree.' Raoul's tone was tight. She could tell that he was as angry as she was.

'No wonder it's taking Paulie time to get over what happened. The trauma of it. . . .'

'Yes,' he said, a little absently. And then, 'Trisha, look!'

Bewildered, she stared up at him, and saw that

he was looking towards the mouth of the cave. She followed the direction of his gaze. And then she saw it—a jaw, sharply pointed, and open. It pointed downward, then lifted. Trisha gasped and clutched at Raoul's arm as she let out a gasp.

As Raoul took a step towards the horrible thing she tried to pull him back. 'Raoul, no!'

'This is it, Trisha!' And then gently, as he became aware of her fear, 'Don't be frightened. Don't you know what it is?'

She went with him as he walked to the opening of the cave. Unashamed, she held on to him as they came into the moonlight—and then she gasped again.

A bush grew by the cave, one of its branches sharply forked, extending beyond the opening. Its shape was that of an animal's long pointed jaw.

'It's like a shadow game,' Trisha whispered, thinking of the games she had played with Jerry when they were children, moving hands and fingers making animal shadows against a light wall. 'Raoul, it's incredible!'

'And so simple.'

'How did you know?'

'I didn't. But I guessed there was something . . . some illusion.' His voice hardened. 'They saw Paulie was taken in by an optical illusion and they played on her fear.'

'They told her it was a wolf. . . .'

They were almost at the station-wagon when Trisha said, 'There's something I don't understand. Paulie heard it bark and howl.'

'Recorded sound. I've no doubt that when we

come back here in the daytime—because we will bring Paulie to see this bush—we shall find a few old batteries in the scrub. If the kidnappers weren't behind bars I think I'd kill them. Trisha, you're trembling.'

'Delayed shock.' Her voice wobbled. 'And it's so cold out here.'

'At least you have your story.'

'Yes,' she said dully.

'For myself, I shall go on believing that you came because you thought I'd be in danger.' He hugged her to him. 'I'll make you warm, my lovely daredevil.'

He opened the door of the station-wagon and climbed in beside her. Then he turned her to him, pulling her across his lap. His mouth began a whispering path along her cheeks, moved to her ears, then made an erotic exploration of her throat. Beneath his touch she felt quite drugged for what seemed long moments. It was only as his hands went beneath her sweater, when she felt his fingers on her breasts, that her senses leaped to vivid life. He began to kiss her, deep hungry kisses, and she pushed her hands against him, sliding in turn beneath his sweater, and then she was touching him, loving the feel of the hard chest, the pulsing strength of his throat. There was exultation in what she was doing; never before had she experienced a joy and a sexual freedom quite like this.

The fires inside her grew fiercer, the longing to be even closer to him greater than she had ever dreamed possible. The last remnants of sanity

deserted her. There was just the wish to be part
of this man. Even if there was no future with
him—as there could not be—she loved him, and
this night belonged to them alone.

It was Raoul who held back. Pushing her a little
away from him, he captured her hands in his.
'Trisha,' he said, his voice ragged, 'I don't want
it to be like this.'

'Raoul. . . .' The whisper was a plea.

'Not like this, dearest, on the seat of a station-
wagon. And there's Gary. . . .'

Gary. Did he really think there was anything
between her and Gary? Trisha was numb as Raoul
moved behind the steering wheel and turned the
key. She pulled down her sweater and ran a distraught hand through her hair, then huddled as
close to her side of the car as was possible.

If she had heard the word 'dearest', the endearment had no significance for her. There was just
the sense of rejection. Raoul had never worried
about Gary before, why now?

She glanced at him as he drove. The strong
profile was set, determined. In the last days there
had been gentleness in him, but there was no
gentleness now. She thought he looked angry, and
she did not know why.

Was this how it was all ending? When Paulie
had seen the forked branch they would return to
Vareen House, and Trisha would go back to
Durban. There was nothing more to hold her
back. Even Paulie, her ghost laid, would need her
no longer. Gary would find a new girl, and Raoul
would be with Salina.

And where would she be? Trisha wondered. The Vareens would live as they had always done, though more happily now. What of herself? She had a job which no longer seemed appealing. A friend—she could hardly call George a lover—who would have lost what attraction he had once had for her. A brother who needed help. At least Jerry would get what he wanted, for she knew now how to rescue him from his mess. Carl and George and Jerry would all get on without her. But what of herself? In such a short time the world that had been hers, and settled, had been shattered. There was no way she could return to it. What would she go to instead?

'Cold again?' Raoul asked once, glancing at her.

She was very cold, a coldness that came from within and spread through her body. 'Not really,' she said.

'We're almost at camp.'

The headlights picked up the tents as the station-wagon pulled up by the tree. Raoul and Trisha were getting out of it when a figure came out of the darkness. 'Where have you been?' Gary's voice was taut with anger.

'We went to the cave,' said Raoul.

'At night?'

'I had a theory about Paulie's wolf.'

'One that could only be tested at night,' Trisha put in, 'and it worked, Gary. A branch. . . .'

'Together?' he interrupted. She thought he had not heard what she said. 'Why did you go together?'

That question was difficult. To tell Gary the truth would be to fuel his jealousy. She looked at Raoul, then said, 'One person had to be outside the cave, the other inside.'

Gary was silent a moment, then to his brother he said 'I could have gone with you.'

'Leaving the two girls to sleep here alone? No way, Gary.'

'Well, I suppose in the circumstances. . . . But I don't like it, Raoul, I really don't. You and Trisha always. . . . What did you find anyway?'

'We'll show you in the morning.' Raoul was matter-of-fact. 'It's very late now. Time for us all to get to bed.'

In the early morning the gorge looked different again. The craggy rocks had the look of a moonscape and the thorny bushes were softened with the sheen of dew. There was even a kind of beauty here, Trisha thought, an eerie haunted kind of beauty which she would remember a long time.

Paulie was amazed when she saw the forked branch, disbelieving too. 'That can't be it,' she protested, shaking her head.

'I think it is. Watch while I move it.' Raoul made for the mouth of the cave. 'And try to imagine the sound of howling.'

Paulie's face changed as she saw the branch slowly lift, then descend. It was an innocent-looking thing in the light of day, but Trisha had seen how it was transformed at night.

'Paulie?' Raoul called from outside.

'Yes. . . .' Clenched hands relaxed very slowly.

'You're right. Gary! Trisha!' She looked wildly from one to the other. 'It *was* the branch!'

'Sis—oh, Sis, I'm glad!' Gary was at her side, his arm going around her shoulder. 'Now the dreams will stop.'

'I hope so.' Paulie's voice was low. After a moment she said, 'How can people be so cruel? I was so frightened. There was no way I could have escaped. What did they get out of it?'

'Some perverse kind of pleasure,' Raoul said grimly. He had come back into the cave in time to hear the question.

'It's over, Sis,' said Gary. 'You can forget everything that happened.'

'It won't be easy. . . .' Paulie was still very pale.

'But it *is* over. Gary's right.' Trisha gave the young girl a warm hug. 'You can start living again.'

'Yes.' Paulie's lips trembled. She began to cry quite suddenly, a heavy weeping, as if at last she was free to vent her feelings of unhappiness and fear and despair—a different sound from the way she had cried after the nightmare. Her brothers stood by, tall and uneasy. Trisha put her arms around the girl and held her, and gradually the weeping ended.

'I want to leave here,' said Paulie, lifting a tear-stained face. 'I don't want to see this place ever again.'

CHAPTER NINE

'I'M going back home tomorrow.' Trisha made the announcement—it sounded like an announcement even though she had spoken in her most casual tone—in the lovely dining-room when dinner was almost at an end. Three faces turned to her, and on each the expression was different. Raoul's face, the one which concerned her the most, was blank.

'We've had so little time together,' Gary protested.

'Can't you stay longer?' Paulie asked wistfully.

Only Raoul said nothing. Trisha took a sip of wine and wished the throbbing at her temples would still.

'I must go back,' she said firmly. 'You've all been very kind, but I think I've overstayed my welcome.'

'Oh no!' Paulie cried. 'I couldn't have come through all this without you.'

Trisha's eyes went to Raoul, who held them steadily. She turned back to Paulie. 'Thank you'—her voice was as gentle as she could make it—'but you would have managed just as well with your brothers.'

Silence fell at the table. Trisha was searching for something more to say when Gary said loudly, 'You're not going!' All eyes were on him now as he stood up. Apprehension quivered through Trisha as she saw him flash Raoul a defiant glance. Then, moving closer to her, he put his hand on her shoulder. 'Trisha is going to be my wife,' he said.

Trisha stared at him, dazed. Even through her confusion she saw the defiance in Gary's face. You're doing this to annoy Raoul, she thought. It has nothing to do with me.

She opened her mouth to say something, and found the words did not come. On the periphery of her vision there was Raoul. His eyes were hard, his jaw a set line. He had not moved a muscle, yet somehow Trisha got the impression that he was very angry.

'No!' she got out. 'No, Gary.'

The hand on her shoulder tightened. 'Yes. I want you to be my wife, Trisha.'

'This is an awful mistake.' Somehow she got the words out. 'Gary, I'm sorry. . . .' Shaking off his hand, she fled from the room.

Gary found her in the garden. She was leaning against a low wall, staring out over a vista of orchards. 'Trisha, I didn't mean to upset you.' His voice was low.

'Why did you do it?' She looked at him with eyes that were wide and unhappy. 'Why didn't you speak to me first?'

'I should have—I'm sorry.' He sounded very unhappy. '*Will* you marry me, Trisha?'

'No, Gary, no. I meant what I said.'

He took a step towards her. 'I love you.'

This was going to be difficult. 'You think you do,' she said very gently.

He took hold of her shoulders, his hands digging into the soft skin of her shoulders. Trisha had to force herself not to flinch. 'I do love you,' he insisted.

'No, Gary. We . . . we get on well together, but . . . but what you feel for me isn't love.' She put her hands on his face, clasping it on both sides. Oh, Gary, I'm so sorry this has happened. But you'll forget me, once I leave here you'll forget.'

'You don't like me at all?' he asked low-toned.

Why couldn't he leave it? This was just agony for them both. 'Of course I like you,' she said.

He was silent a moment. His hands loosened, and she thought he was going to release her, then his hands tightened once more, biting with painful cruelty this time. 'It's Raoul. Raoul's after you.'

She shook her head through a blur of tears. 'No. . . .'

'I've seen you together—always you and Raoul. Last night, when you got back from the cave together, it was the final straw.'

Through a blur, she asked, 'That was why you talked about marrying me?'

'No!' And more slowly, 'Yes. . . . But only in a way. I do want you, Trisha.'

'You only think you want me,' she said softly. 'We're not right for each other, Gary. I could never make you happy, as Yvonne would do.'

'Yvonne?'

'She loves you. Didn't you know?' She lifted her hands to his and pried his fingers from her shoulders. Then she rose on her toes and kissed him swiftly on his lips. 'I shall never forget my stay here. Be happy, Gary.'

Early next morning Trisha phoned for a cab. She had said her goodbye to Gary last night in the garden, she did not intend to repeat it. Paulie was awake when Trisha knocked on her door.

'I'd have loved to have you for a sister-in-law,' she said wistfully when Trisha said she was leaving.

'It wouldn't have worked.'

'With Raoul, perhaps. You seemed to get on so well together.'

'Raoul has Salina,' Trisha said briskly.

'I suppose he has,' Paulie said thoughtfully. 'Any day now they might . . . though sometimes I wish. . . .'

'I must be going,' Trisha cut in, unable to endure any more. 'You'll be all right now, Paulie?'

'Oh yes. Now that I know. . . . Thank you for everything.' She threw her arms around Trisha who felt a wet cheek against her own. 'Will we get together?'

'Yes. Yes, we will.' But they would never meet again, Trisha knew. The break with the Vareens must be final if she was to endure it.

Her eyes were wet too as she made her way out of the house with her suitcase in her hand. She was glad to see the taxi waiting at the foot of the steps. She got in quickly, and breathed a sigh of relief as the vehicle pulled away.

She had not said goodbye to Raoul. Once before she had postponed her departure; this time she would not wait to see him. There was no longer a promise binding her to Vareen House. And she did not think she could bear to say goodbye to the man she loved.

The next days were mercifully busy, leaving her little time to think of Raoul. Her first call was at the office, where Carl Samson received her eagerly. 'That was some extended stay with the Vareens,' he said, leaning back in his chair and smiling at Trisha expansively. 'You must have quite a story.'

'It is quite a story,' she said slowly.

'When will you have it ready for us?'

'Mr Samson . . .' Trisha took a deep breath, 'I'm not giving it to you.'

'What!' The smile vanished as the editor sat upright in his chair. 'You're not serious?'

'I am.'

'You couldn't be doing the dirty on us? Giving the story to someone else?'

'You don't understand. I've decided not to write the story.'

'Damn right I don't understand!' he snapped. 'This is a scoop, Miss Maxwell. Not another paper has managed to get a word about Paulie Vareen. What's got into you?'

'Shame, remorse.' Her head was throbbing. 'I didn't want to insinuate myself into Vareen House in the first place. I only did so because . . . well, because Jerry needed the money. . . .' She stopped.

'Go on.'

'I got to know the Vareens. Paulie is sweet,

vulnerable. She's been through an awful ordeal, Mr Samson.'

'The public have a right to know about it,' he insisted.

'I don't believe they do.' Momentarily there flashed through Trisha's mind a picture of Raoul; how zealously he had defended his family's right to privacy. 'Paulie has suffered enough, and she has rights too.'

'You phoned me from Vareen House. You said you wanted to stay longer, that you'd be getting a story.' Hard eyes studied her across the paper-littered desk. 'Something must have happened to change your mind.'

I fell in love. Madly, crazily in love. I discovered that I have certain principles and that I want to live by them.

'Something did happen,' she said slowly, 'but I don't want to talk about it.'

'Be careful, Miss Maxwell,' he warned. 'You work here.'

'No, Mr Samson, I don't. That's one of the things I came to tell you.'

She was rising from the chair when he said, 'What about your brother? The money you needed?'

'That will be taken care of.'

'The Vareens are helping you?' He looked at her incredulously.

'I'm helping myself.' She held out her hand. 'Goodbye, Mr Samson. I enjoyed working here.'

Sally, her friend and flatmate, was surprised and upset when she learned that Trisha was leaving. She sat at her typewriter, hair rumpled, eyes that were normally merry now serious. 'Aren't you rushing things, Trisha?' she queried.

'I don't think so.'

'You've really made up your mind?'

'Yes, Sally, I have. We'll talk later at the flat.'

'Trisha,' a hand went out to detain her, 'what will you do?'

'I'll manage.' A smile that was braver than she felt. 'See you later!'

In the street once more the smile vanished. Would she manage? What would she do? Yes, she *would* manage; she had no other option.

She had looked up an address in the telephone directory, then began to make her way along the hot Durban streets. But outside the shop with its three gold-coloured balls swaying in the wind, she hesitated. What joy would she get from a pawn-broker? Surely she could do better than that.

She began to walk once more. When she stopped again it was outside a jewellery store, one that had a reputable name. Trisha watched anxiously as the owner studied the emerald. He lifted his head once, looked at her, then back at the lovely green stone.

'Where did you get this?' he asked at length, looking at her once more.

'It's an heirloom.'

'I see.' His face was carefully bland as he went on to tell her how much he would pay for the piece.

Trisha considered the offer. It was less than the stone was worth, she knew, but it was also as good as she was likely to get. Apart from paying Jerry's debts, she would have enough money to support herself until she decided on a new career.

Parting with the emerald was surprisingly difficult. She had not realised it meant quite so much to her. Though she had not worn the pendant more than a few times, she had cherished it in memory of her grandmother. As she watched the man place the stone in a special case she felt a thickening in her throat. It was silly to feel that she had severed a link with someone she had loved very much. Gran would have been the first to approve her decision. 'Better that you let it make life easier for you than you keep it locked away in a small box.' Blue eyes would have glittered with humour. 'It's just a stone, darling.'

Nevertheless, as Trisha walked out into the glare of West Street, Durban's main downtown road, she had to blink away the tears.

Twice she went to Jerry's apartment; it was only at the third try that she found him in. His relief at the sight of the money was both naïve and annoying.

'Sis—oh, Sis, thank you!'

'You have to stop being gullible, Jerry,' she said, as firmly as she was able.

'I've promised,' he assured her.

'Do you know how many times you've done that?' She sighed. 'Jerry, I've given up my job.'

'Trisha!' He stared at her.

'I'm going to have to tighten my belt a little.' She laughed at his face. 'Not that it's ever been very loose. The point is, you can't go on depending on me.'

'I'll be good—honestly, Sis.'

The words were said with such good humour that Trisha could not remain angry with him. Jerry was all the family she had left and she loved him, no matter that he was irresponsible. He meant the promise sincerely, she knew that; the question was how long he would keep it.

'What on earth are you going to do?' Sally asked, eyes wide with consternation later that evening.

'I'll find something.'

'Modelling?'

'I don't know.'

'Gary Vareen thought you were the real thing.'

'Yes, well. . . .' Carefully Trisha poured coffee into two cups. When she looked up again the tension she felt at the name Vareen was concealed. 'What I'd like,' she said, 'is to open a gift shop.'

'You're crazy! There are so many in Durban.'

'Not in Durban, somewhere along the coast. I'd try to steer away from the usual kind of merchandise, Sally, go for local things. . . .'

'You need money for a shop,' Sally pointed out.

'I have some. I don't know if it will be enough, but, Sally, I'm going to give it a try.'

They were tidying the kitchen when Sally said, 'Been in touch with George since you got back?'

'. . . Yes.' There had been a call with George, an awkward call that Trisha wanted to forget.

'You've dumped him?'

'We've agreed . . . not to . . . to see each other for a while.'

'Well, how about that!' Sally spoke with an eagerness of which Raoul would have approved had he but heard her. 'Too pompous for you, Trish. By the way, did you ever hear from that dreamboat?'

A cup clattered to the floor. 'Damn thing slipped out of my hand,' Trisha muttered. 'Didn't break, though.'

'Did you hear from him, Trish? You must remember, the fellow you met when the kid was knocked from his bike?'

'Sort of. Do you want me to leave the coffee in the percolator for breakfast, Sally?'

'Might as well. You don't sound too excited. If you run into dreamboat again give me a shout— there's one man I'd like to meet!'

Four days passed during which Trisha walked around gift shops and craft shops. She looked through books in the library, and took a drive along the north coast road, stopping at holiday resorts and fishing villages. She had not found what she wanted, but her mind buzzed with ideas. 'You're on the run all the time,' Sally said once, 'and you come back looking exhausted. Can't you give it a break, Trisha?'

Her room-mate did not know that she welcomed exhaustion. For a while at night she would lie and think of Raoul—during the day she kept herself deliberately too busy to let her mind wander—but mercifully sleep did not take long in coming. In the mornings she would wake knowing she had dreamed of him, and she would get out of bed filled with a wrenching sadness.

Would she ever stop thinking of Raoul? Probably not. But the hurting that went with it, how long could it last? No man is worth crying for, Sally often said, perhaps because she had never loved deeply. Trisha sensed that her own weeping, a silent weeping deep inside her, would continue a long time.

She returned from the library one afternoon, her arms full of books. Balancing them on one arm, she put her key in the lock and saw that it was open. Was Sally home? It must be later than she had thought.

'Sall...' The call stopped in her throat, and standing just inside the door she stood rigid. Someone was in the flat, but not Sally. And there was something—an aura of a sort—that she recognised.

'Sally,' she said again, tentatively this time, more to reassure herself than because she still believed her friend was in the flat.

'No,' said a deep attractive voice, as Raoul came through the living-room to meet her.

'How...how did you get in?' she asked shakily as he took books from her arms.

'The caretaker opened the door for me.'

'He shouldn't have.' The words seemed to emerge quite mechanically through the sensations that flooded her at his nearness.

'Of course not. Aren't you going to come further in, Trisha?'

'Yes. . . .' Watery legs found direction some-how, and carried her into the living-room. 'Why are you here, Raoul?'

'You didn't say goodbye to me.'

'And that's why. . . . Raoul, you were angry?' She stared at him, thinking that he was even more handsome than she had remembered him.

'Furious!' His voice was rough. 'I'd have come the day you left, but it's taken me this long to get certain things settled.'

Raoul here, and angry, and implying that he would have liked to come earlier. Trisha shook her head in confusion. Raoul would have been glad to see the back of her, would have been relieved that the girl who had done so much to disrupt the atmosphere in his home was gone. None of what he said made much sense.

'What things?' she asked after a moment.

'For one thing, a talk with your boss—yes, I went to see Carl Samson. And he told me something I'd suspected.' The eyes that lingered on her face were narrowed, and his voice had hardened. 'Why didn't you tell me you had no intention of writing the story?'

'You wouldn't have believed me.'

With one swift step he closed the gap between them and clasped her face in his hands, sending familiar fires shooting through her nerve-stream. 'You always did think you knew what I was thinking, didn't you, Trisha?'

'You . . . you said for one thing. . . .'

'Ah. It took me two days to track down a certain jeweller.'

With her face in his hands it was impossible to look away from him. If he were not so angry she would let her fingers trace every craggy line of the beloved face.

'You found out about the pendant?'

'And bought it back.' A hand left her face as he took the pendant from his pocket.

'Why?' She stared up at him through eyes that shone no less than the emerald.

'Because it should never have been sold. Your grandmother gave it to you. One day you'll give it to your daughter—if not your granddaughter.'

There will be no daughters, no sons either. Don't you know that I couldn't bear to marry anyone but you, and you're as good as married to Salina.

But there was no time to pursue the thought, for on the heels of it came another. 'You shouldn't have done it,' she said a little desperately. 'That money ... I needed it, Raoul. Jerry ... my brother ... now he'll have to....' She covered her face with her hands as the implications of Raoul's action crowded in on her.

Gentle fingers pried her hands loose from her face. 'I do think of consequences,' a dry voice said. And as she stared at him in confusion. 'I've been with Jerry too.'

'No!'

'I told you I had a number of things to see to.' Mobile lips curved in wry amusement. 'I tracked down your young brother, and we had quite a talk—among other things.'

'The money!' Trisha exclaimed in sudden

understanding. 'He would have had to return it now that you've got back the emerald. But you. . . . Oh no, Raoul, you shouldn't have!'

'In the circumstances it was right that I should.'

At the look in his eyes Trisha caught her breath. There was no time to think as he went on, 'Jerry understands that he has to rely on himself from now on.'

'He tries, but he doesn't seem able. . . .'

'He will,' Raoul said with quiet firmness. 'He knows he'll have my help if he needs it.'

Green eyes fluttered open, wide and luminous. The tall man studied them a moment, and in the rugged face was an expression of intense satisfaction.

Questions tumbled on Trisha's lips, but she did not know how to frame them, did not even know if she dared. Raoul seemed to know how she felt, for he said, 'You haven't asked about Gary and Paulie.'

'Do they know?'

'About the model who was really a naughty reporter?' Blue eyes sparkled. 'I had to tell them.'

'Were they very shocked?'

'An understatement! But by the time I left home they were beginning to get over it. I think Paulie was actually rather amused. As for Gary, Yvonne was doing her utmost to make him feel better.'

'Do you think they'll get together, Gary and Yvonne?' she asked.

'I hope so. Yvonne is an extremely sweet girl.'

The sparkle intensified. 'Pliant too. She'll be just right for my brother. Unlike you, my stubborn daredevil.'

There was an odd softness in his tone. Even the word 'daredevil' had the sound of a caress, as it had had once before. And that was surely absurd, for waiting at Hazeldene was Salina.

'Will Gary forgive me?' Trisha asked.

'I think in time he will.' Raoul laughed softly. 'He can hardly bear a lifelong grudge against his sister-in-law, now can he?'

Joy was a wild thing in her chest, her throat. 'What . . . what did you say?'

'That you and I are going to be married.' One hand went to her chin, cupping it, so that he could look down into her face, while the other hand went around her waist, drawing her to him. 'Trisha, my darling, you will marry me, won't you?'

She shook her head dazed. 'But you hate me.'

'I love you, my naughty, adorable daredevil. Don't you know that?'

Such joy after so much unhappiness—it was almost too much to take in. There were questions, many questions. But they would have to wait for another time. And there would be time, Trisha knew suddenly—much time. Just one question had to be asked now.

'Salina? What about Salina?'

'She was never more than a friend. A very good friend, but nothing more. And she knows about us. I told her the evening we went out for dinner. But Trisha, you haven't answered me. *Will* you marry me?'

'Oh yes, my darling, yes!'

She was in his arms then, and he was kissing her, deeply, hungrily. Somewhere a door was heard to open, there was the muffled exclamation, 'Jumping jellyfish, the dreamboat!' and then the door closed again. 'I love you,' Raoul said, lifting his head just for a moment, and then his mouth came down for another kiss.

HELP HARLEQUIN PICK 1982's GREATEST ROMANCE!

We're taking a poll to find the most romantic couple (real, not fictional) of 1982. Vote for any one you like, but please vote and mail in your ballot today. As Harlequin readers, you're the real romance experts!

Here's a list of suggestions to get you started. Circle your choice, <u>or</u> print the names of the couple you think is the most romantic in the space below.

Prince of Wales / Princess of Wales

Luke / Laura (General Hospital stars)

Gilda Radner / Gene Wilder

Jacqueline Bisset / Alexander Godunov

Mark Harmon / Christina Raines

Carly Simon / Al Corley

Susan Seaforth / Bill Hayes

Burt Bacharach / Carole Bayer Sager

_____
(please print)

_____

_____

Please mail to: Maureen Campbell
Harlequin Books
225 Duncan Mill Road
Don Mills, Ontario, Canada
M3B 3K9

POLL-1

What readers say about Harlequin romance fiction...

"Harlequin books are the doorway to pleasure."

"They are quality books—down-to-earth reading! Don't ever quit!"

"A pleasant escape from the pressures of this world."

"Keep them coming! They are still the best books."